all of us strangers

TAICHI YAMADA

TRANSLATED BY
WAYNE P. LAMMERS

MARINER BOOKS

NEW YORK   BOSTON

ALL OF US STRANGERS. Copyright © 2003 by Taichi Yamada. English
translation copyright © 2003 by Wayne P. Lammers. All rights reserved.
No part of this book may be used or reproduced in any manner
whatsoever without written permission except in the case of brief
quotations embodied in critical articles
and reviews. For information, address HarperCollins Publishers,
195 Broadway, New York, NY 10007.

HarperCollins books may be purchased for educational, business,
or sales promotional use. For information, please email the Special Markets
Department at SPsales@harpercollins.com.

Originally published in Japanese as *Ijin-tachi to no Natsu*
by Shinchosha, Tokyo, in 1987.

First US edition published as *Strangers* in 2003 by Vertical Inc.

FIRST MARINER BOOKS PAPERBACK EDITION PUBLISHED 2024.

Library of Congress Cataloging-in-Publication Data has been applied for.

ISBN 978-0-06-341152-4

$PrintCode

all of us strangers

After my divorce, I set up house in the apartment I had been using as an office.

Since I made my living writing scripts for television dramas, I spent most of my waking hours in solitary confinement at the apartment. Until recently, I had a lady friend who came here to share her company with me, but she drifted away when I became caught up in the divorce proceedings with my wife. I didn't mind; I had expended so much emotional energy on the divorce that I was perfectly happy to be free of human entanglements for a while, including those whose pleasures were of a purely physical nature.

One night about three weeks into my life of renewed bachelorhood, it hit me how quiet the building was. Too quiet, I thought.

Not that the place was a secluded mountain retreat. Quite the contrary, the seven-story apartment building faced directly out onto Tokyo's busy Route 8, which never saw a break in traffic no matter what time of day.

When I first began living here full time, in fact, the endless noise kept me awake at night. Large, long-haul trucks timing their trips for the midnight hours when traffic wasn't so heavy sped by one after the other, and the rumbling roar seemed to well forth from deep within the earth. Lying in bed prey to this din, I would feel short of breath. With a stoplight only a hundred meters or so down the road, the noise periodically came to a halt, only to rend the silence at an even higher pitch a few moments later as the trucks ground into motion again. The relentless thundering would resume, my heart would beat harder and harder, the walls would close in, and I would bolt upright gasping for breath.

It took me about ten days to get used to the round-the-clock barrage.

When I'd contemplated spending the night at the apartment, back in the days when it was still only my office, I had dismissed the idea out of hand, knowing I would never be able to sleep. But with my bank account drained after the divorce, I could not afford to move anywhere else; having no choice but to take up residence here, I soon discovered that one could indeed adapt even to conditions such as these. The incessant roar of traffic retreated to the far reaches of my consciousness, as did the hum of the air conditioner, and I would sometimes realize in surprise that the *tock tock tock* of the second hand circling the clock on the wall had become the only sound I was aware of.

But now it had reached the point where the building seemed altogether too quiet, and I had to wonder where my own senses were leading me.

This feeling of too much quiet first came over me on a night near the end of July as I sat working at my desk a little after eleven. A chill ran down my spine, and I felt as though I were suspended in the middle of a vast dark void, utterly alone.

2

"It's awfully quiet," I murmured.

I ignored the feeling for a time as I continued to write. After a while I reached for the dictionary to look up a kanji character I couldn't quite remember, and as I flipped pages in search of it, I realized that the same uneasy sensation had been gnawing at me for the past several nights.

I stopped turning pages and listened. Through the roar of traffic I strained to capture some other recognizable sound. I could hear nothing.

Had my divorce left me with unresolved anxieties of some kind? I wondered. Who in their right mind would think that a building overlooking a major traffic artery was too quiet?

I had asked for the divorce myself. And even though my ex-wife had raised all manner of objections at first, she soon conceded that the principal emotional bond uniting us had become indifference. The truth was, she too felt an emptiness in our marriage and, once she had had some time to think about it, she wholeheartedly embraced the idea of divorce. We did hit some rough spots on the way to the financial settlement, but no one would have termed the divorce a messy one. At the very least, compared to muddling on endlessly in a lifeless marriage, donning the same old benign faces day in and day out as we went about our lives together but apart, the decisive action had awakened in me a whole new zest for life.

"I'm so glad you suggested it," my wife had gushed in the end. I was not so foolish as to take the remark entirely at face value, but it must have contained at least some element of truth. At any rate, since I was the one who had asked for the divorce in the first place, I could hardly complain about loneliness now. *So what* if it was too quiet?

Rising to my feet, I stepped to the window and drew the curtains aside. I left the window closed. It was not sealed, so I could have opened it if I chose, but I knew that would serve only to let in the relentless heat of the day, along with the thick fumes and undampened roar of the traffic racing back and forth along Route 8.

I dropped my eyes to the parking lot. I couldn't see the entire lot from where I stood, but I already knew how many cars I could expect to find.

Just one. Save for a single pink van parked by itself, all I saw was a broad asphalt emptiness broken only by a grid of white lines. The spaces all filled up during the day, but as darkness fell, the vehicles began to vanish one after another, leaving only the pink van behind. I had seen it there last night, too.

Last night, too? That's right, I realized. Last night, too, I had stood at the window like this, gazing down at the asphalt emptiness below.

Was I suffering perhaps from not seeing my only son, who was a college sophomore this year? It seemed unlikely. After all, I had already withdrawn to my own little world long before the divorce. If I had been fine with almost never seeing my son then, why should I suddenly start missing him now?

I picked up my keys from the pencil tray on my desk and dropped them into my pocket on my way to the door. As I stepped out into the seventh-floor hallway, I left the lights on. I didn't want to believe that the feeling I had of the building being too quiet came from a weakened state of mind, and

I intended to find out once and for all. I wanted to prove that the building really *was* quiet—because it was effectively empty. No one actually wanted to live in such awful apartments, bombarded day and night by the din and fumes of traffic speeding by. The only tolerable use for the place was as office space.

The hall-side windows of the other four units on my floor were all dark. I pushed the button for the elevator.

I had known that some of the apartments were being used as offices, but I had not expected quite that many. Apparently, most of the building's occupants departed at nightfall. If I remembered correctly, the building had forty-one units altogether; probably all but one or two per floor were empty at night.

The elevator doors slid open. The compartment was empty.

I'd always hated the moment when elevator doors opened in buildings like this one. I shrank at the thought of abruptly coming face to face with a complete stranger. When the compartment proved to be empty, I breathed a little sigh of relief.

I stepped in, and the elevator descended to the first floor. As I emerged into the unair-conditioned lobby, thick, muggy heat washed over me. I made my way through the dimly lit lobby and pushed my way out the front door.

Outside, the air was filled as ever with the noise and exhaust of passing vehicles, but the descent of darkness had taken some of the edge off the day's heat. I headed for the parking lot.

Two more sedans were parked in spaces not visible from my window. The pink van I'd seen from above had three smiling squirrels painted on its side, and I learned that it was a sales van for a company that made children's apparel.

I threw my head back to study the building's southeast face. Every apartment had at least one window on this side. I could reasonably expect to see a light wherever someone was home.

Only a single window showed any light—my own, on the seventh floor. Every other window was completely black.

"Wow," I let out in surprise.

I stood contemplating the rows of darkened windows. Far from one or two per floor, there were no overnight occupants at all. At this hour, after eleven, only my own window was lit up. I wasn't being neurotic; the building really was silent. Possibly some of the windows were dark because the residents had already gone to bed, but I doubted that could account for more than a few units.

I slowly strolled back to the entrance feeling vindicated.

Entering the building was not quite as easy as exiting. You had to insert your apartment key in the security panel on the wall next to the door. A turn of the key disengaged the lock for about twenty seconds. So long as someone was home, you could get into the building without a key by using the intercom. A button got you through to the desired apartment, and once you had identified yourself, the occupant could unlock the door for you by pushing a button in the apartment. In that case, too, you had about twenty seconds to open the door and enter the lobby. Since the building manager always went home at night, this was apparently considered all the security the building needed.

So I'm the only one here, I thought as I went inside. I'm the only one left in the entire building.

Even though I still could not be completely sure, part of me actually wanted to think so. I walked across the lobby to a sofa set against the wall and plopped down heavily. It did feel a little spooky to think that I was all alone in such a large building late at night, but it was also liberating—as if I had returned to my childhood and its innocent, exciting sense of freedom.

I had not been sitting there more than a minute or so before I heard someone approaching the entrance. My heart skipped a beat, and I instinctively scrunched lower on the sofa.

The sound of footsteps reached the door and stopped. Slowly turning my head, I could see through the glass that it was a woman. I studied her as she rummaged inside her purse for her key. She did not appear to be especially young—perhaps in her mid-thirties.

She inserted her key in the security panel as I had done myself only a minute or two before, and I stiffened a little. I was afraid I might startle her, since she certainly would not be expecting to find anyone sitting in the lobby at this hour. The lock disengaged and the door opened. I lowered my head. Her heels clicked rapidly along the floor as she hurried toward the elevator. A pair of white shoes and shapely legs strode across the periphery of my vision. The rhythm of her steps did not falter, so she apparently had not noticed me. If so, all the better.

Without pause she stepped into the waiting elevator, and

the doors slid shut with their usual mechanical sound. I lifted my eyes toward the elevator, then quickly rose to my feet. The light over the doors came to a stop on the third floor.

Four or five days later I got a call from Mamiya, a producer at one of the TV stations I sometimes worked for. It was evening.

"Do you mind if I drop by?" he asked.

Mamiya and I were the same age, forty-seven, and we had worked together on and off for nearly ten years, sharing credits on six different projects. Of those, a two-hour special and two drama series had taken their place among my most important works—titles that I always included even in the most condensed résumés of my career. Because of these successes, though he had other qualities to recommend him as well, I was fond of him. Even the somewhat stiff reserve he showed seemed to agree with my temperament. After all these years of working together, he still never brought up anything about his private life, and he always remained polite and correct with me.

"I apologize for intruding on you with so little notice," he said with typical formality.

"Not at all, not at all. Please come in."

I was delighted to see him again. He had not approached me in nearly a year. My standard practice was to fill up my schedule on a first-come first-served basis as the calls came in. Even if I thought a more attractive job might come along if I kept myself open, I almost never turned down an offer if there was room in my schedule. So, even though I had been hoping I could work with Mamiya again sometime soon, I had already filled my plate for the coming months. You sure took your sweet little time, I felt like grousing, but all the same, if I could possibly swing it I was inclined to accept whatever work he brought my way, even if it meant stretching myself a bit thin.

There was an actor we both regarded as one of our finest, who tended to get unruly when he drank. One night when we were drinking at a club in Aoyama with four or five others, though perhaps unruly isn't quite the right word in this case, he started doing a striptease. It wasn't really that kind of an establishment, and the shocked looks of patrons at tables nearby made it obvious that someone needed to put a halt to it. I hesitated for fear I might make him fly off the handle. But suddenly Mamiya was on his feet. I assumed he was going to try to stop the striptease, as I'm sure everyone else at our table did. Instead, Mamiya started dancing with the man. And as he danced, he, too, began tossing off his clothes. Before long the two of them were taking turns belting out lines from bawdy songs, and through it all, Mamiya seemed completely in his element. I was utterly flabbergasted to discover that he could be that way. As it happened, that was neither the first nor the last time he had done something that caught me by surprise, and each time I felt like I'd discovered something new to like in him. He lived alone—at least that was what he told everyone. Rumor had it that he owned a small airplane and spent most of his free time out at the Chofu airstrip, but I'd never heard Mamiya himself say anything about such a hobby. When we met, he spoke only of the work at hand. Since this was not uncongenial to me, I too started to consciously avoid talking about my private affairs. And Mamiya never asked me about them, either.

As a result, on that particular evening when Mamiya sat at my table watching me retrieve a large bottle of beer from the refrigerator and asked how I was managing my meals, I actually felt as though he was wrecking our relationship. It was not the kind of thing I wanted to discuss with him.

"I saw your two-hour special the other day," I said, trying to change the subject to one of his recent projects.

"I hear you never show up for anything anymore," Mamiya responded.

Ignoring this, I remarked that I had really enjoyed the special. "I'm glad," he said as I poured him some beer, but he refused to crack a smile. He took just one gulp of his beer and set his glass down.

"Don't tell me this is a sympathy call," I said.

"Oh, by no means." He finally showed a hint of a smile.

"For a moment there I wondered if looking grim was required protocol on visits to divorced men."

"Not at all."

"What is it, then?"

"Well . . ." Mamiya averted his eyes.

"Bad news of some kind?"

When a television producer suddenly shows up on a writer's doorstep, you can be pretty sure it's not good news: The slot for the drama we've been developing has been given to a quiz show. Our ratings are down, so our series is getting the ax. Our leading man has been arrested for drug possession. Our leading lady just got married and refuses to kiss anyone but her husband, so can you rewrite the scene without any kissing? That sort of thing.

But since I had no current projects with Mamiya, I had no idea what he could be looking so grim about. Then he spoke.

"Shouldn't you be seeing more of your son?"

It came as a bolt from the blue, like the lash of an undeserved reprimand. My mind attempted but failed to find the connection between Mamiya and my son. I tried not to show my unease.

"Where's this coming from?" I asked.

"I saw your wife the other day."

No doubt he meant he had run into her somewhere by chance. I inwardly grimaced to think what she might have told him about our divorce. This was the man with whom I had tried so hard to set private matters aside.

"Are you here on some kind of an errand from her?"

"No. It's just . . . I was just wondering if it wouldn't be better to establish certain rules, like seeing your son once a month and things like that. It's not her idea at all. I was just wondering."

I was taken aback at the earnestness with which he said this, the color rising a little in his cheeks.

"I suppose if my boy were still a kid in junior high that might make sense," I said. "But he's nineteen. He's perfectly capable of coming by on his own any time he wants."

"But what about you? Aren't there times when you'd like to see him?"

12

"I can't say there aren't, but he'd probably roll his eyes at a once-a-month rule. If I think back to when I was nineteen, I know I'd have been pretty bummed out if someone told me I had to sit down to dinner once a month all alone with my father."

Mamiya nodded. He seemed to see my point.

"But you know," I continued, "this is very gratifying. You caught me by surprise there for a minute, but it really is gratifying. I never expected you to be so concerned for me over something like this. I mean, I had you pegged for the type who prefers to steer clear of all that domestic stuff." I lifted the bottle and topped off his glass. "But the truth is, I'm as fond of domestic intrigue as the next guy. All this time I've been thinking I wanted to avoid the whole scene of people worrying about me, but now that you've seen fit to speak up, I have to say I'm gratified. Though I *am* disappointed that you're not here to talk about work."

"Actually, there's that, too."

"Oh," I said, jumping to conclusions. "Well, of course there is! It'd be silly of you to come all this way just to ask about my son. What sort of project did you have in mind?"

"I didn't mean it that way."

"What then?"

"I came to tell you I won't be able to work with you anymore."

"You're getting out of producing?"

"No."

Mamiya sat perfectly still, keeping his eyes averted.

"I don't understand," I said, forcing a smile. "I hope

13

you're not telling me that getting divorced is cause for cutting a writer loose."

Mamiya didn't answer.

"I think I deserve some kind of an explanation," I pressed. Without something more from him, I couldn't make heads or tails of what this was all about.

Mamiya's lips parted a little and he seemed about to say something, but he immediately pressed them firmly back together. His jaw started trembling as though he were fighting to keep the words from gushing forth. When he finally opened his mouth again he did so very deliberately, as if to warn: Now listen very carefully because I'm only going to say this once.

"I want you to know I intend to start seeing Ayako."

Ayako was my ex. I understood the words he had spoken, but they didn't sound quite real. They were simply too far removed from anything I could have expected to hear.

"Seeing Ayako?" My voice betrayed my puzzlement.

"Now that I know you're divorced, I can no longer contain my feelings. I hope to marry her."

It was a decidedly odd feeling to hear someone else expressing such an ardent interest in the woman with whom I had chosen to sever ties. On the one hand, I wondered if perhaps I should be kicking myself for my foolishness; on the other, I felt like I knew that the man sitting before me was about to make a very wrong turn but that I could give him no effective warning.

"I see." I could think of nothing else to say.

"Right." That was all Mamiya offered.

14

I could not recall the tiniest hint from Ayako of anything like this while we were going through the divorce. Then, almost as if he had read my thoughts, Mamiya looked up and said, "Ayako doesn't know."

The nerve of the man, throwing Ayako's name around so lightly! Okay, so he might feel a little strange referring to her as "your wife" under the circumstances. But he could at least show a little sensitivity and stick with a simple "she." And did he really expect me to believe that she didn't know?

"Right," I said. "Of course not."

That had to be their story anyway. Otherwise how could Ayako justify squeezing me for all I was worth in the settlement? But here Mamiya was, barely a month later, telling me he could not contain his love for her. Nothing could convince me that she really didn't know.

"You may think it's no concern of yours since you're divorced now," Mamiya was saying, "but I thought it might not be quite that simple."

In other words, since I had divorced Ayako, it was none of my business what he might do with her. And since he had nevertheless had the courtesy to come and seek my blessing, so to speak, I should acknowledge his wishes and butt out. That's what he really meant.

"So at this point, you haven't given her any indication of how you feel about her?"

"Uh-huh," he replied, leaving a note of ambiguity.

"Then it's possible she won't want anything to do with you?"

"That's right."

15

"In that case, coming to seek my blessing at this stage is taking common courtesy a bit far, don't you think?"

"You've been a very important person to me."

Overblown and vain words. Clichés like that got tossed around like pocket change in the entertainment world. With some people they could have the desired effect, so I had no objection to using them in the context of business, but it stung like a slap in the face to hear such a line from Mamiya concerning a strictly private matter. I was so "important" to him that he wanted to forego working with me so he could get it on with Ayako. He sat there with a look of great anguish, but he actually felt no pain at all. He felt no regrets at cutting himself off from me. It was all a game to him. He was merely amusing himself by barging in and saying these things to me. And what was more, he remained completely oblivious to what he was actually doing. Mamiya, of all people, had come to tell me that he had placed my writing and my ex-wife on scales and that the balance had tilted to her.

A profound sense of despair came over me, and I felt a sob rising in my throat. I rolled my head back and gazed up at the corner of the room, pretending to examine some cobwebs I'd been neglecting.

"Though surely she will rebuff me," Mamiya said, sounding rather like a stilted subtitle.

"I don't know why you should think that."

He had to have worked everything out with Ayako already. He said he'd seen her, after all, and obviously something had come up about our son. In other words, she had kept mum about carrying on with another man so she could squeeze every last bit she could out of me.

But whining about that now would be the worst, and flying into a rage would leave a sour taste as well. I would have to find another way of showing him I was onto their dirty tricks.

"Let me express my deepest gratitude for all you have done for me in the past," Mamiya said very formally.

"Not at all," I answered mechanically. It was all I could do to keep from exploding.

"I'm terribly sorry," Mamiya said with a deep bow, then added, "I think I'd better be going. It's too painful to . . ." He sounded on the verge of tears.

Good grief! I inwardly rolled my eyes. This is turning into a regular soap opera. What happened to all our efforts, on and off screen, to avoid such sappy treacle?

But Mamiya had crossed on over to the other side, all the way into the world of melodrama. "Good-bye, then," he said, rising to his feet and performing another deep bow.

"Good luck," I heard myself saying stupidly. At this rate, I would soon be joining Mamiya on the other side.

"I hope you can forgive me," Mamiya blurted out as he fled for the door.

Everything seemed to follow the rules of conventional melodrama. Now he was putting on his shoes. When he was done, he would stand erect and act like he had one last thing to say. But he'd be too choked up to speak, so he would simply give another little bow and turn to the door as though shaking himself free of the emotions bottled up in him. This

17

was how it was done in the hackneyed world that he and I had tried so hard to avoid.

I watched as Mamiya performed exactly as I had anticipated. The door closed behind him.

After what had transpired, I was hardly in the mood for more company that night.

The apartment remained exactly as it had been when Mamiya departed. I had neither grabbed his glass and thrown it at the floor in a fit of pique, nor calmly turned my attention to preparing and eating dinner. Rather, I had simply wandered into my bedroom—the only other room in the apartment besides the one that doubled as living room and study—and flopped down on the bed. I was still there, listening to some music on FM, when the intercom chimed.

I glanced at the clock on my nightstand and saw that the time was 10:24. Who could it be at such an hour? No one from the stations I currently had dealings with ever dropped in unannounced. The security system at the main entrance downstairs generally thwarted door-to-door salespeople; now and then one of them managed to slip in after a resident had passed through, but then they usually got turned away when they announced themselves through the intercom at the individual apartments, so I couldn't imagine that they did much business. There were, of course, quite a few people who knew my address here, and theoretically any one of them could have chosen to drop in, but nobody I could think of was likely to come without calling first. A possible exception was the lady friend who used to visit me here, but given

18

how we'd parted, I doubted I would ever see her again. We had not been a particularly good fit, she and I, even as sexual partners.

I picked up the handset to the intercom. "Yes?"

"Hello."

It was a woman's voice, but not one that I recognized.

"Who is it?"

"I'm at your door. I live in the building."

The intercom made the same sound whether the visitor rang in from the security panel at the main entrance or from the hallway right outside the door. That was why she had felt the need to clarify.

"Just a moment, please."

I sighed wearily. I didn't know whether she wanted to hit me up for a contribution or ask me to sign a petition, but I was in no mood for anyone's spiel. Even the note of youthfulness in the woman's voice failed to dispel my annoyance. But I didn't suppose I could just leave her standing there, either.

I opened the door.

"Oh."

It was the woman I had seen pass through the lobby several nights before.

"I hope I'm not disturbing you," she said. She wore a cotton housedress, pale green with a large, boldly sketched flower on the front. Of course she was disturbing me, but I couldn't very well say so.

"What is it?"

Her face was unnaturally white. Her makeup seemed a little too heavy for a woman in a housedress.

"Did you know?" she said, as if trying to pique my interest in a choice morsel of gossip about someone.

"Did I know what?"

"That by around this time most nights," she said, averting her eyes, "you and I are the only two people left in the building?" Her eyes returned to meet mine.

I felt a rude jolt, like I had been bitten by a centipede. When a woman learns she is alone in the building with a strange man, wouldn't the more normal response be to double-lock her door and offer up the most vigilant guard she could muster?

"No," I said in a tone that suggested I could hardly have cared less.

She averted her eyes again and seemed to be bracing herself against the icicles in my voice. Had I been my usual self, I might have hastily added a warmer remark of some sort to make amends, but I was in a foul mood that night. I stood there without a word.

"That's all," she finally said, her tone suddenly forlorn.

She thrust a paper bag at me that contained a bottle of some kind.

"A little something to mark our new acquaintance," she sniggered self-derisively. Then quickly, as if to banish her snigger, she added in a much brighter voice, "It's champagne. A half-empty bottle of champagne. I opened it, but I couldn't drink it all, so I thought maybe I could share it with you. If I keep it until tomorrow, it'll just go flat."

She giggled gleefully.

"That's very kind of you, but . . ."

I forced a smile but did not move.

"Oh, I'm not celebrating anything. It's nothing like that," she said. For the first time, she sounded a little drunk. "It's just a bottle someone gave me a couple of years ago. I happened to come across it the other day and put it in the refrigerator thinking I'd go ahead and drink it, and tonight I finally opened it. I'm drunk, aren't I? I get tipsy right away. A third of a bottle and I'm completely sloshed." She giggled again. "Otherwise I wouldn't dare do something like this. Anyway, do you mind?"

"Excuse me?"

"Do you mind if I come in?"

Yes, I certainly did mind. She was an attractive enough woman, but I bristled at her brazenness—asking such a thing without the least regard for my convenience. I was still groping for what to say when she spoke again.

"I just couldn't help myself," she blurted out as if with her dying breath. "I have no idea what came over me, but tonight, as I sat there in my empty apartment, all of a sudden I couldn't stand being alone anymore, so, I don't know how many times I changed my mind, but, in the end, I decided to come. I mean, think about it. In the middle of the night, there's only one or two of us in the whole building. It's scary. I'm on the third floor. You could come to my place instead if you'd like."

The alcohol seemed to be making her a little crazy.

"I'm in the middle of a rush job."

My foul mood had reasserted itself. The gall of the woman! Not the woman standing before me now, but the woman I had claimed as my wife until barely thirty days before.

"You're working?" the woman standing before me was asking.

"Pardon?"

"You're working right now?"

"Yes. I'm trying to wrap up a rush job."

After demanding our six-year-old house and the land it was built on as well as the securities I'd made the mistake of placing in her name and all of our savings, Ayako had made a grand show of generosity in front of the arbitrator by saying, "I suppose he'd like to make a clean break, so I won't ask for educational expenses for our son." Lo and behold, Mamiya had been lurking in the shadows all along.

"I see," the woman before me was nodding.

"Huh?"

"If you have to work, I guess this isn't a good time."

"I'm afraid not."

"Please forgive me."

"No need to apologize." I reached for the doorknob.

"Oh," she exclaimed, but I closed the door before she could say she still wanted to leave the champagne with me. Even as I watched her image vanish, my mind had already turned elsewhere. Renewed anger at Ayako and Mamiya swelled like a massive wave within me. I sent the deadbolt home with a loud *clack*!

I returned to my bed and turned the radio back on.

Almost immediately a feeling of unease crept over me.

My mind raced. Maybe I should have asked her in after all. When a person suddenly shows up talking like that, don't you have to figure something pretty serious is going on? Or was that true only for me, and for her it was nothing more than a lark? Then again, she also said she didn't know how many times she had changed her mind. What if she does something rash because I gave her the cold shoulder? What if her crushing loneliness makes her kill herself?

Oh, get a grip! I told myself. She isn't going to die. Her face didn't have anything like that written on it.

I got up and opened the door again. The hallway stood empty. I listened for telltale sounds, but all I heard was the roar of the traffic rushing by outside.

I'm sorry, but I simply don't have time for other people's troubles right now. I've got too many of my own.

Making lame excuses, I retraced my steps to the bedroom.

I could not sleep. I poured myself a nightcap of whiskey.

Thoughts of the woman continued to tug at me as the alcohol slowly took its effect, but for the most part my mind did battle with the shock dealt me by Mamiya and my ex-wife.

Morning arrived. Daytime noises gradually brought the building back to life. The hollow clicking of heels on concrete floors, first in one direction, then another. Doors latching shut. Telephones ringing. People's voices. The rising tide eventually reached next door as that apartment, too, began to stir with the activities of office staff going casually about their day's business, and the next thing I knew it was almost noon. I really ought to make sure the woman is all right, I told myself, but I was too weary to do anything about it.

3

I ran into the woman two days later in the lobby.

It was a rainy afternoon, and I saw her coming into the building as I stepped out from the elevator on my way to a meeting at a TV station.

She carried an umbrella in one hand, and a purse and two or three bulging plastic grocery bags dangled from the other. She noticed me.

"Hello," I volunteered. I was feeling apologetic.

"I'm so sorry about the other night," she said with a polite bow, her voice a little squeaky. "It was terribly rude of me, at such a late hour." When her head came back up, I could see a tinge of embarrassment hovering about her eyes, and she seemed much prettier than before.

"I wasn't exactly on my best behavior either."

"I'm sorry to have bothered you when you were rushing to finish a job."

"Please don't mention it. If you'd be so inclined, I'd like to invite you for drinks again some other time."

"That's very kind of you. I'm really so embarrassed."

Saying good-bye, we went our separate ways. Some leafy greens caught my eye in one of her grocery bags as I slipped past her toward the entrance.

I breathed a small sigh of relief, but at the same time I felt a little bit like I'd had the wind knocked from my sails.

Shortly after ten the night before, I had made my way outside to see if there were lights in any of the third-floor windows. It was raining. I found one bright window each on the first, third, and fifth floors. No silhouettes appeared in the third-floor window.

Naturally, I realized that a lit window didn't necessarily mean anything. She could easily be lying cold on the floor with her lights blazing away.

I stood in the rain and watched the window for a while. In the end, I went straight back to my apartment without seeking better verification, but dire thoughts about the woman and her deep loneliness had continued to weigh on my mind.

Now, after all the worry I had put myself through, a plastic grocery bag with greens peeking from its top brought me back to reality.

I should have known better, I thought with a wry grin as I made my way toward the station. People aren't so eager to do themselves in most of the time.

Then came the fateful day—a day in early August.

I still wasn't getting out much. I didn't attend parties or go barhopping with friends. I'd never been the gregarious type to begin with, and now the divorce proceedings and the Mamiya shock had turned me downright antisocial.

When I bumped into the woman in the lobby, I'd suggested she might come over for drinks sometime, but as the days drifted by I never quite felt like calling her. She didn't call me, either.

Of course, invitations like that often mean nothing more than "It's good to see you" or "It was nice talking to you." In the entertainment business, lighthearted promises and hollow assurances are as commonplace as breathing, and everybody knows they aren't intended to be taken seriously.

"One of these days we should go drinking when it has nothing to do with work, just for fun."

"For a chance to work on one of your projects, I'd turn down all other comers in a snap."

"There's no question about it; if something isn't done soon, the Japanese TV drama is going down the drain. Someday you and I should put our heads together and reverse that."

"Say, why is it I never get cast in any of your shows? I have? Oh, that's right, that was your script, wasn't it? Silly me, I'm such a doofus. I just lo-o-oved that show. It was so awesome. I'd never dug so deeply into a character before, not for TV."

In eighteen years of making my living as a scriptwriter, I had learned not to test the sincerity of such pleasantries.

My neighbor on the third floor was not in the entertainment industry, of course, but she belonged to essentially the same urban culture. I doubted she could navigate her daily existence completely free of empty compliments. And besides, suppose I did invite her to come over. What could we possibly have to talk about? I had no interest in listening to her prattle on about her work or her private life or her past. A sexual relationship might be agreeable enough if it could stop at just that, but I flinched to think of getting caught up in all of those troublesome emotions.

27

And so to the fateful day in early August—August 4th, to be exact. Late that afternoon, I picked out a necktie at a department store in Ginza.

"It's for a gift," I told the thirtyish sales clerk.

She selected four or five ties from inside the glass case and arranged them on the counter. They all seemed a little too dark and subdued to me, and I said so.

"You did say the person was in his forties?"

"Yes, late forties."

"In that case, I don't think he'd find these too subdued, but let me see . . ." She quickly selected another four or five ties and laid them on the counter. This time her selections were so flashy I almost winced at the glare.

"How about something halfway between these and those?" I said.

She apparently didn't understand the sort of thing I had in mind. "Such as?" she asked.

"Something that's neither too restrained nor too loud," I said as I began scanning the entire selection in the glass case myself. I soon saw that I was seeking the impossible; I was asking for something they did not have.

It hit me then that my efforts to make something of the new independence I had gained were much the same. I flailed about, unable to put my finger on exactly what it was that I wanted, dissatisfied with what seemed too sober, recoiling from what seemed too wild, looking for something that simply did not exist.

In the end, even though I doubted I would ever actually wear it, I left the store carrying a flashy cream-colored tie

28

with bold swaths of orange and yellow and green splashed across it.

I was disgusted with myself for having said it was a gift. A man my age giving himself a necktie for his birthday—how pathetic was that? Sentimentalism of that sort would never even have occurred to me in my younger days, and it was certainly not the kind of thing I cared for anyone to know about.

Sometimes, traveling abroad, I had thought how much more my horizons might expand if I only knew the local language. I could talk easily with anyone I met. I could seduce women.

But in fact, I knew that no matter how fluent I became in the language, I'd still find myself trapped in the straitjacket of my own nature, too reticent either to strike up casual conversations with strangers or to win favor with women. By the same token, getting divorced wasn't likely to expand the horizons of an over-forty television writer so terribly much. I knew this.

"I know that's true, and yet . . ." I murmured quietly to myself.

Evening had begun to descend on the city. The oppressive heat that had held the city in its grip since morning seemed to have left behind a thin film of grime on everything it touched. As I walked along the sidewalk bathed in the sticky air, I found myself resisting the inclination of my feet to turn directly toward home.

I could see myself arriving back at the apartment and taking a shower, then sitting down to work in air-conditioned comfort for two or three hours. That would lighten my load the next day. Afterwards I would lie back on the sofa and sip at a glass of whiskey while I watched a Fellini film or some such on video. In other words, my evening would be exactly the same as the previous.

I yearned for something a little different, and not merely because it was my birthday.

I realized I had sunk into a kind of depression. Somehow, I needed to pull myself out of it. I needed to get on with my new life. From that perspective, buying a necktie as a birthday present to myself represented just about the worst possible state of mind.

I stopped short. Something had caught my eye—though I wasn't immediately sure what.

I found myself standing before the entrance to the Ginza subway station. The sign over the descending stairway said "For Shibuya and Omotesando. For Asakusa and Ueno," indicating the two directions that particular line could take me.

Asakusa. That's what had brought my feet to a halt. It seemed like I hadn't seen that name in ages.

Asakusa was my birthplace.

That's it! I decided on the spot. I'll visit Asakusa. Now that I finally knew where I wanted to go, I trotted quickly down the stairs.

Quite a few years had passed—quite possibly more than a decade—since my last trip to Asakusa.

I had been born there in 1939, the first child of a sushi chef and a kitchen helper working at the same restaurant. We lived in an apartment close to the Tawara-machi subway station. My father served two stints in the army, one before I came along and one after. Toward the end of the war, with my father still away, my mother and I went to stay with my grandparents at her childhood home in Tochigi, north of Tokyo. Once the war ended and my father was repatriated from the Philippines in 1946, we immediately went back to live in Asakusa. My parents threw together whatever edible items they could get their hands on and sold it in the black market as "Vitamin Stew." I was in grade school at the time, but I often helped out, too. I remember watching my mother thicken the stew by mixing flour and water in a large bowl and stirring it into the great big bubbling pot. Steam from the pot billowed up around her youthful face.

My father finally found regular work again as a sushi chef around the time the Korean War broke out in 1950. The shop was in Nihonbashi, but both my parents liked living in Asakusa, so we continued renting there. Our apartment was on the second floor of a tinsmith's house behind Honganji Temple.

It was there that my mother became pregnant with her second child.

Sadly, though, I never found out whether the baby would have been my little brother or my little sister.

In January of the following year, my father was riding my mother on the back of his bicycle when a car plowed into them in front of the International Theater. Both of them died on the spot. The hit-and-run vehicle was never tracked down.

My uncle in Nagoya speculated that it must have been a jeep belonging to the American Occupation, and that was why the police couldn't pursue it, but I was told at the time of the accident that they'd been hit by a black sedan.

Having lost both of my parents at the age of twelve, I went to live with my widowed grandfather in Aichi, in the farming village not far from Nagoya where my father had grown up. Our small acreage failed to produce enough of a harvest to take to market, so we mostly just ate what we grew. I suppose my grandfather felt sorry for me; he seldom asked me to help with the farm chores. But I worked hard at becoming a regular country boy. I knew I'd better wipe away all signs of my city upbringing as quickly as I could if I wanted to make it through the local junior high unscathed.

I was orphaned again when my grandfather died in the middle of my junior year. My uncle came to dispose of the farm, and afterwards I went to live with him in Nagoya during my last year and a half of high school.

For college, I returned to Tokyo. My uncle told me not to worry about a thing, he would send me the money I needed to get through school. When he passed away a number of years later, a distant relative who came for the funeral suggested that he had cheated me by sending me far less than I was entitled to, but I found it hard to imagine that my grandfather's meager lands had sold for a particularly large sum, so I have never questioned my uncle's generosity.

The passengers thinned out considerably at Nihonbashi, and more got off at Kanda and Ueno. By the time the subway reached the end of the line at Asakusa, only three or four passengers remained in each car.

I climbed the stairs that led in the direction of Kaminarimon Gate and emerged into the thickening dusk. Contrary to what I had anticipated from the emptiness of the train, I found the streets and lanes in the area brightly lit and bustling with pedestrians.

After passing through the massive gate, I strolled between the shops flanking the approach to Sensoji Temple. I was okay with visiting the temple and the entertainment district immediately to its west, but I remained reluctant to extend my tour to those sections of Asakusa most intimately linked with my childhood memories. In all my previous visits, I had never once turned my steps toward the International Theater, or the streets around Honganji Temple or Tawara-machi Station. This being Tokyo, I knew that no matter how far removed they might be from the center of Asakusa, those neighborhoods could not possibly look much like they had more than thirty years ago, and yet I remained fearful of venturing into them.

I dreaded, for example, what might happen if I were to find still standing the tinsmith's place where my parents and I had spent our last days and months together. The emotions I had dammed up inside me all these years might come bursting through the floodgates in an uncontrollable deluge.

I had allowed myself few tears since my parents' death when I was twelve. But if I were to walk again along the streets and lanes I had known as a child and in doing so came upon something that vividly reminded me of my time with my parents there, it could snap every last cord binding the armor that had been protecting me; I could be stripped naked and collapse in a blubbering mass of tears.

Grow up and stop whining! I chided myself. Besides, you know perfectly well that the International Theater gave way to a large modern hotel ages ago.

Dropping a ¥100 coin into the offering box at the front of the temple, I put my hands together and closed my eyes. A flash of light enveloped me, and when I turned to look, I saw an elderly Caucasian man lower his camera, watching me a little nervously as if worried he might have offended me. I smiled and nodded at him, and he seemed relieved. He said something in English and waved his hand.

I left the grounds through a side entrance near the temple's main hall. The pedestrians were far fewer here, and so were the lights. As I headed in the direction of the movie theaters, a man sidled up to me and matched his steps with mine.

"Looking for a good time, mister?" he asked in a raspy voice.

"No thanks, I'm on business."

I looped back to the street in front of the ward office and stopped for some supper at an eel restaurant. It was past seven-thirty by the time I finally set foot in the theater district.

A forlorn air hung about the area. Seven or eight theaters remained in business, but the street was nearly deserted. Given the hour, perhaps this was to be expected, since the last shows of the day would already have begun. But I also remembered how empty the streets had been even at midday the last time I came, and that made me wonder if the place always had the atmosphere of an old forgotten byway these days.

Suddenly a tall, brightly lit building loomed before me. With a small plaza out front that set it back from the street, it seemed to materialize out of nowhere. It had not been there on my last visit.

Housing a variety of specialty shops, the building would have fit right in in Shibuya or Kichijoji or any other bustling shopping district, but it seemed rather out of place in its actual surroundings. It clashed sharply with the shabby old structures nearby, creating the impression that a building belonging to an altogether different dimension had somehow gotten plunked down in that spot by mistake.

To me, this bright, sanitized building was a greater scar upon the townscape than the closed and boarded-up theaters or the bare lots that remained where buildings had been torn down. I suspected, though, that this impression was destined to fade as the entire area transformed itself to match the style of this new building.

Another pimp sidled up to me.

"Got a real cutie, mister. Only eighteen. Great ass."

"I just finished."

"Ah, very good, sir. Please come again."

The unexpected politeness of his response made me turn to look at him. I was surprised to see him flash me a friendly smile as he backed away.

Most of the time when you told the pimps who approached you like this that you weren't interested, they turned away without a second glance, so I had not expected him to still be looking at me. Not only that, I was disarmed by his smile, which contained no hint of the "Sure, I bet" sarcasm such men typically showed, and I found myself instinctively smiling back.

A moment later I halted my steps. I realized that if I proceeded all the way to the end of the street where it ran into the Toei Cinema, I would see the International Theater off to the left. Or rather, I would see the high-rise hotel that the International Theater had been torn down to make way for. I wanted to avoid that. I decided to turn back.

As a child I had not actually seen much of the International Theater's famous high-kicking line-dancers, of course, but the building had loomed large as a backdrop to my daily comings and goings until the age of twelve. And the final memory of my childhood in Asakusa was the sight of my parents' blood staining the pavement of the wide boulevard that ran in front of the theater, a short distance down the street toward the Tawara-machi subway station.

The next time I stopped, I was standing in front of the Asakusa Variety Hall. The comic monologue then in progress was being piped outside through a speaker by the entrance. The doors were still open, but no one was going in; I was the only person who even paused at the entrance.

I pictured the hall within to be sparsely filled. It might be fun to take in an act or two before heading home. Because of the late hour, admission had been reduced from ¥1,500 to ¥1,000.

To my considerable surprise, the hall was packed. Even

36

the stools set out for additional seating were mostly taken, and a number of people were standing. I would never have anticipated such a lively, charged atmosphere from the way the place had looked outside. Laughter erupted from the audience in great bursts as the young raconteur milked every comic nuance from his narrative.

The monologue went on for another four or five minutes before concluding to a rousing ovation. As the clapping began to taper off, an announcement came over the speakers.

"Members of the Shopkeepers Association and the Dove Tours group are asked to please return to your buses now."

All at once, the vast majority of the audience got to its feet and began crowding into the aisles to make for the doors.

As a television writer, I, too, performed for an audience, in effect, but I had never had to witness this kind of exodus. Watching the audience depart as though nothing could stop them was like seeing my worst nightmare come true.

The orchestra struck up some music to announce the beginning of the next act, and a new raconteur appeared. Even after he had taken his place on the cushion at center stage, the departing patrons still clogged the aisles, pressing for the exits.

"Thank you so much for coming," the mid-fiftyish story-teller cried after them in a high-pitched voice. The audience still seated laughed. "Yes, indeed, that's the way out, folks, so please hurry, hurry, hurry to your buses. Thank you so much for coming." Collapsing nearly prostrate, he repeated with feigned sobs in his voice, "Thank you so much for coming."

The exodus continued unabated. "Right that way, folks. That's the way out for those who wish to depart." He put on a show of weeping and sticking his tongue out in chagrin. "I worship Dove Tours!" he cried. "When you get back home, please be sure to brag to your friends that you caught a glimpse of me, too."

The hall finally fell silent again. The remaining audience was sparse.

"Dove Tours can be so cruel," the performer sighed. "This is just between you and me, now," he said, lowering his voice secretively, "but Dove Tours gets those folks in for half price. ¥750 per person. So before you go getting too stoked about the turnout, you have to remind yourself that it takes two of them to be worth a full admission. And then they hop up and walk out on you like that—without a moment's pause or regret. They hear the call to their buses and boom, boom, boom, it's a stampede for the doors. I can't stand it. I'm sorry, but to tell you the unvarnished truth, I can't stand Dove Tours."

He intended this all in jest, of course, but it came off sounding a bit too serious, and an awkward tension filled the air. Then a voice broke the silence.

"They're still here, you know."

My heart skipped a beat.

The raconteur grew flustered. "No! You're pulling my leg, right? It's not true, is it?"

"Just kidding," the same voice said. The audience burst into laughter.

"Why, you dirty scoundrel, you! Now, *that* was cruel. My liver stopped pumping. No-o-o, I mean my heart, not my liver. I *lo-o-ove* Dove Tours, I'll have you know. Honestly, I do. I'm their biggest fan. Good grief! You shouldn't go around teasing people about matters of life and death. It's Dove Tours that puts the vittles on my table."

The lead-up to his monologue was turning into quite a rap session. "I don't reckon I should be mouthing off to those of you who stayed behind, but it's a big-time bummer to get up here on stage and see three-quarters of the audience hiking toward the doors. Makes you wanna pack up and go right on home yourself."

I rose from my stool at the back of the hall and moved to a seat several rows forward.

"Hey, there, mister, don't scare me like that," the performer said, looking directly at me. "Didja really have to get up just when I thought I'd managed to patch the breach in the dike? I was about ready to run down there and grab you by the sleeve and beg you not to go—until I realized you were actually coming forward, thank you very much. Please, by all means, make your way down front. No need to stop there. Come right on down where you can feel my spit fly."

The audience was laughing again, some watching the man on stage, some looking at me.

At that point the raconteur steered his unbroken chatter toward a new topic. He started poking fun at some television celebrities.

I had not changed seats to get a better view of the act. In fact, I had no good reason to change seats at all. It was a silly thing to do.

Though I did not immediately look in his direction, I had changed seats to get a better angle on the man who'd said "They're still here, you know." From my previous spot, I'd been able to see only the back of his head.

The man's voice and his rear profile had reminded me uncannily of my father. Of my dead father. And for that reason, a sudden impulse had taken hold of me: to move to where I could see the man from the side.

But so what if the man did remind me of my father? What was the big deal? My father died at the age of thirty-nine, so if he were alive today, he would be seventy-five. Had something about a man of that age reminded me of him, my behavior might have made more sense, but this character looked like he must still be in his thirties. There was something just a little off kilter about my response.

To avoid drawing any more attention to myself than I already had, I made a point of laughing along with the rest of the audience, but I heard almost nothing the raconteur was saying. I wanted desperately to turn and look at the man. His voice had sounded astonishingly like my father's. And his bearing from behind had looked heart-wrenchingly like images of my father that remained etched in my mind. That was why I so wanted to see his face: I wanted to see it and assure myself that he did not really look so much like my father in the end. After all, no one could resemble my father in every respect. I sought the healthy dose of disappointment that would quiet my racing heart.

The monologue came to a close.

I turned to look at the man. It was my father. Or rather, it was a man whose profile was the spitting image of my father at the time of his death.

Wow! I thought, quickly looking away. I'd never have believed that two different people could look so much alike.

The orchestra signaled the start of the next act, and a husband-and-wife juggling team swept onto the stage.

I could not find the courage to look toward the man again. I'd seen him for no more than a second, I noted to myself. Plus, I wasn't really all that close. What basis did a glance give me for judging how much of a likeness there might be? The man would probably look completely different if I saw him from the front. That sort of thing happened all the time.

Now I felt like I just had to see him from the front, and I could hardly contain myself. But I knew perfectly well it would be pointless. There was no way my father could be walking around Asakusa today.

On stage, the husband was balancing a ball on the tip of a cane, which was in turn balanced on his forehead. He stepped left, then took several quick steps to the right to keep the ball and cane from falling.

As I followed him across the stage with my eyes, I stole another peek at the man.

He was looking back at me.

My heart stopped. The man smiled and dipped his head in a little nod. My flesh went cold. Averting my eyes, I stared at the floor and tried to quell my extreme agitation.

Why would he be looking at me? Why would he smile and nod as if he knew me?

But of course, it was because the storyteller had given me

41

such a hard time when I switched seats a while ago. Something had probably reminded him of that and made him wonder how the guy who got needled was doing, and our eyes met when he looked my way. The smile meant nothing more than an offhand "Enjoying the show?" He just happened to be an amiable sort of guy. The pimp who came up to me outside seemed like an affable fellow, too. That's what's nice about Asakusa. You can still run into people like that around here.

At any rate, now that I'd actually seen the man's face, what was the verdict? Well, how was I to know? My father died when I was twelve. I could hardly claim a precise recall of every little nook and cranny of his face. Sure, he looked like my father, but just how much had to remain open to question. All I could really say was that he was the spitting image of my father as my increasingly vague memory—with the help of some old photographs—had pictured him through the years. He was a dead ringer. Even when our eyes met, I could have sworn I was looking at my father. Yet, that did not alter the fact that he could in no way actually be my father.

The juggling act concluded to tepid applause.

So why was I getting so worked up over nothing? By now, he probably thought I was a strange one, too. He'd offered me a smile and my only response was to turn my eyes away. He might even be feeling a little offended. "Yo," I heard a voice say very close by.

I looked up to find the man standing in the aisle at the end of my row.

"Whadda ya say we get outta here?" he said.

"Are you talking to me?" My voice trembled. He was indeed the living image of my father.

He started for the door without waiting for me to respond. His receding figure betrayed not the slightest doubt that I would follow. The orchestra signaled the beginning of another act.

I rose from my seat and hurried after the man.

4

Outside, the nighttime theater district lay virtually deserted. The man stood waiting for me to emerge from the building.

"I can't stand this guy," he said, poking at the playbill on a board propped up next to the entrance. Just then, the voice of that raconteur started crackling from the speaker.

"I don't like him much, either," I said.

"Course not." The man started walking. "He ain't cut out to be a closer, that's for sure."

We were headed in the direction of International Boulevard.

"Wanna stop by?"

"Excuse me?"

"You wanna come by the ol' place?"

The man shifted his hips as he hiked up his pants.

"Are you sure it's all right?"

"Of course it's all right. What're you talking about?"

I gauged him to be at least ten years my junior, but he was dispensing with all formalities as if he were talking to a much younger man.

"The trouble with Asakusa nowadays is how the whole place closes down so early. Can't find anythin' going on anymore after ten."

We came out onto International Boulevard and stood waiting for the light to change. The street was still a major thoroughfare, but it did not seem as wide as I remembered it. Traffic was light.

"D'ya come often?"

"Excuse me?"

"To Asakusa, I mean."

"Now and then."

"Yeah?"

He marched briskly across the pedestrian stripes. I followed. People like this usually rubbed me the wrong way, but I couldn't bring myself to part company with him. He fumbled for something in his pocket as he crossed the street.

"I'm gonna fetch me a pack o' smokes," he turned to say. "We'll be going that-a-way. Just wait here, all right?"

Instructing me to hang tight by the crosswalk, he jogged somewhat bowleggedly up the sidewalk in the direction of the International Theater—where it had once been. A cigarette vending machine stood facing the sidewalk, and I watched as he started inserting coins. The man wore a white Henley-necked shirt hanging loose at the waist over a pair of white cotton pants. His short-cropped hair gave him a sharp, clean-cut image. I had been feeling a measure of relief over this fact—I suppose because I didn't want a man who so resembled my father to look seedy.

He started back toward me.

"So whadda ya think?"

"Excuse me?"

"The hotel. It's huge, don't you think?"

"Ahh, yes," I agreed, though from where we stood, the

row of nearby buildings blocked my view, and I could not actually see the hotel that I knew had replaced the International Theater.

Apparently unconcerned with such minor details, the man set off again in the opposite direction. I fell in a half-step behind.

I found myself walking easily through a section of town I had not set foot in since the age of twelve. Now that I was here, it seemed like any other time-worn neighborhood in what had once been Tokyo's bustling merchant quarters.

By all indications, we were on our way to this man's home, and it seemed odd even to me that I was following along without the slightest hesitation. It would have been understandable if I had been in an advanced state of inebriation, of course, but I was not. What could have possessed me, I wondered, to let this stranger I had scarcely met take me to his home?

The answer was simple, of course: he bore an astonishing likeness to my dead father. This likeness had undone my usual sense of caution and rendered me helpless to resist.

Then again, why had this man gotten the notion to take me to his home in the first place? I was obviously much older than he was, so I couldn't very well remind him of his dead son.

"Beer okay?"

"Pardon me?"

He seemed so like my father that I instinctively answered politely—even though I was actually the elder.

"It's hot, so I thought maybe a nice cold beer would hit

the spot," he said, stopping to count the change in his hand. We were standing at another vending machine—this one offering canned beer.

"I only get to keep one bottle in the fridge. 'Cause if I have it, I drink it, you know."

"Let me buy."

"Don't be ridiculous."

Chunk-a-lunk-lunk. A 500 milliliter can dropped inside the vending machine and appeared below.

"It's icy cold. Hold it with a handkerchief or something," he said, handing the can to me.

"All right."

I saw that he intended to buy another.

"Do you think we'll want that much?"

"What're you talking about? It's a coupla measly cans."

Chunk-a-lunk-lunk. Another 500 milliliter can appeared.

"You got it with a handkerchief?"

"Yes."

He took the second can and started off walking again.

"You don't need a handkerchief?" I asked.

"Nah, doesn't bother me."

He seemed quite pleased with himself.

Well, sheesh! It wouldn't bother me, either, I felt like retorting, but an inexplicable feeling of glee welled up in me and stayed my tongue.

I wasn't entirely sure what brought me such glee. But I realized I was relishing every moment I spent with this man, who carried himself with an air of complete authority. I was reveling in the illusion of tagging along after my father. I was

48

basking in a warm sense of security I had not known for a very long while.

It doesn't bother *me*, but I suggest *you* use a handkerchief, he says. What a card!

I restrained an impulse to slap him heartily on the back and let out a great big whoop.

"Here's the place," he said. "Upstairs."

He turned into an alley and immediately started up a metal staircase ascending the side of a small, two-story apartment building. He stepped quickly but softly, taking care not to make noise. I instinctively followed suit.

An open walkway ran the length of the second floor and there were three doors. The man proceeded to the one farthest back.

"It's me," he said, tapping the door with his foot.

I hung back, chills once again racing through my body.

He was married! But *of course* he was. A while ago he'd said, "I only get to keep one bottle in the fridge"—which meant that was all that someone else, presumably his wife, would let him have. Somewhere in the back of my mind that statement had lingered.

I suddenly had this feeling that I did not want to meet the man's wife. To meet her would be to instantly obliterate the glorious time I was having because of the man's uncanny likeness to my father; I would have to come crashing back to reality. No, wait. That wasn't it. Or at least that wasn't all. A part of me was actually entertaining a secret hope, experiencing a secret terror. It couldn't be, could it? Surely it couldn't be.

49

"What're ya standin' way back there for. Come on in," the man said, and disappeared into the apartment.

I remained frozen to the spot.

A woman poked her head out the door. "Do come in," she said, flashing a cheerful smile before disappearing back inside.

I nearly went into a swoon. This couldn't really be happening. There had to be something wrong with me. I knew I couldn't be sleeping, for no dream could be so vividly real and true to life as this.

"Hey! What's the big hold-up?" the man called.

"Please come in," the woman repeated. It was my mother's voice. The woman I'd glimpsed in the doorway was my mother.

My whole body shook. My feet would not move. Choking back tears, I managed to squeeze out only a weak "Uh."

The man stuck his head out the door. "What're ya waitin' for? I told you to come on in."

"Yup . . ."

"Stop being such a mouse."

"Yup . . ."

I struggled to compose myself. I knew I couldn't just turn around and leave. I wasn't ready to break everything off here and never see the two again. Yet it took every last reserve of strength I had to quiet my agitation. Thank goodness being alone in the world for so long had given me plenty of practice at containing my emotions.

I stepped to the doorway and said, "Thank you. I'm sorry to impose at such a late hour."

"Oh, never mind that," my mother said. My mother had

died at thirty-five. But I was gazing at the spitting image of my mother at thirty-five.

"The night is young," my father said. "Here, sit down."

It was a worn-out old apartment with only a small kitchenette and a single eight-tatami room, but it was clean and tidy. They keep a nice house, I noted to myself, deliberately trying to occupy my mind with concrete observations.

The refrigerator didn't look particularly old. Their thermos jar was the modern push-top kind. And, whadda ya know, they had a calendar from "Rox," that new building with all the specialty shops. No way these people were my mother and father.

"Hey, get a load o' this," the man said.

"What is it?"

"It's a controller," he said. "This silly woman is crazy about radio-controlled cars."

Three pretty good-sized model racing cars sat side by side on a sheet of newspaper in the corner of the room.

"She is?" I could not actually look at the woman.

"Can you believe it? At her age? Give her a free moment and she's playing with her model cars. She's already gone through four or five others besides the ones you see there now."

The woman laughed. I forced myself to look at her and saw my diminutive, fair-skinned, slightly thick-lipped mother laughing exactly the way I remembered her laughing.

But the woman played with radio-controlled cars. She couldn't possibly be my mother.

5

I picked up a cab on International Boulevard a little after eleven. The man and his wife saw me to the curb together.

"Don't be a stranger, now."

"Yes, do come again."

I felt like a country boy taking leave of his parents at the train station on his way to Tokyo for the first time. I did not want to say good-bye. Tears clouded my eyes as I watched their figures recede into the distance.

"Some relatives I hadn't seen in ages," I explained to the cabbie.

He did not respond.

"It was really special," I finally added, in spite of his evident lack of interest. Tears wet my cheeks. Perhaps the cabbie thought I was drunk. Well, he was right about that. We had had whiskey after finishing the beer.

The tears felt good. "That was really special," I repeated under my breath. "So special to be back with family after such a long time."

But in truth, the man and woman I'd spent the evening with were neither family nor acquaintance. I didn't know how many times I'd had to stop myself from blurting out the question that kept pushing its way to the tip of my tongue: "You're my mom and dad, right?" At times, I'd even had to cover my mouth.

A thirty-something couple could not possibly be the parents of a forty-seven-year-old man—no, make that a forty-eight-year-old man, as of today. But being with them had made me feel like a boy again. Of course, a boy could not have been drinking whiskey, but in a moment of alcohol-induced carelessness, I had actually addressed the man as "Dad," and he had answered "Yeah?" exactly as if I were indeed his little boy.

The woman, too, had behaved like the proverbial mother hen fussing over her chicks. "Here, spread this hand-towel over your lap. In case you spill something."

"I'm not about to start spilling canned scallops just because I'm a little drunk," I said.

"See? There you go," she said practically with her next breath. "You hardly got the words out of your mouth before you dropped one."

I relived the evening's events as the cab drove along, savoring every sweet moment, every sweet detail. I began repeating aloud all the things they had said to me.

"See? There you go. You hardly got the words out of your mouth before you dropped one."

"Don't be a stranger, now."

"Yes, do come again."

"My goodness! You write for television? You're a big shot then! You even *look* smart."

I'm a long way from smart, Mom, and I'm certainly no big shot. I'm just muddling along all by my lonesome, trying to make the best of my dreary life.

"Don't be a stranger, now."

"Yes, do come again."

The driver had finally had enough. "Hey, mister, watch the spray, will you?" he said. "Keep shouting like that, and I'm gonna ask you to get off."

He could needle me all he wanted as far as I was concerned, but I didn't want to get dumped by the side of the road, so I shut my mouth. Still, I continued to repeat the things the couple had said over and over in my mind.

The city lights glittered all around, and even the traffic signals looked beautiful.

In the haze of a hangover the next day, I doubted that any of those events could actually have taken place. I figured I had dreamed the entire episode after getting drunk and falling asleep on a bench somewhere. But faint vestiges of the sweetness I had experienced still lingered.

At any rate, I needed to get back to reality.

The next four days I spent with the producer and the director of a new television series I'd agreed to write for, tramping all over Tokyo to learn everything we could about what went on in tennis clubs and pool halls. The original plan had been to put together a show about billiards in order to cash in on the game's exploding popularity, but the producer was worried about all the dark interior scenes that would entail. To balance those scenes with brighter locations, he'd hit on the idea of adding tennis as a second focus. I was in no position to argue: my workload was down, and I couldn't afford to jeopardize a chance at landing a long-running series.

At the end of the fourth day, I said good-bye to the production staff at a bar in Ryudo-cho and got home a little after ten. I had agreed to put together a formal proposal—naming the characters, laying out the basic outline of the story, pinpointing the target audience as well as how the show would reach them—and submit it to them two days later.

I turned on the air conditioner and headed straight for the shower. As I toweled off afterwards, I listened to the messages on my answering machine. The first informed me that a two-hour drama I was up for had been canceled. Next came a message from a young actor I knew.

"Um, sorry to keep you guessing for so long, but Ami and I are finally taking the plunge. Yeah, we're gonna be happy together. Ami's talking about a wedding sometime around November in Fiji. D'you think you might be able to make it? We'd really love it if you could be there. Come celebrate with us, Sensei!"

As was the convention between young actors and older writers, he had always addressed me as Sensei even though I'd never been his teacher or mentor. I didn't bother to correct him because I knew it would make him feel awkward, and I would only come off as a snob. Though it seemed rather presumptuous of him to think I might want to go all the way to Fiji to celebrate with them, I supposed that was just how the minds of today's young hotshots worked.

After that came a woman's voice: "This is Miss Fujino, your neighbor on the third floor. I just thought I'd see if you were in. Good-bye."

The air conditioning was finally starting to take effect.

I went to the bedroom to get my pajamas.

It hadn't been much more than ten days since I'd stood in the rain gazing up at the woman's window, and yet, as I listened to her voice now, I felt like I was hearing from an estranged acquaintance whom I'd nearly forgotten.

Since that rainy day, I had been to Asakusa.

My experience there—or perhaps it was all merely a drunken hallucination, but whatever I had gone through that night—had apparently left such a powerful impression on me that everything leading up to it felt like ancient history now.

No, wait, that wasn't quite the full story. Even that night in Asakusa seemed like ancient history to me now. The whirlwind of the last four days had swept aside all that had gone before, and the purely imaginary tale I was preparing to write had taken over every recess of my mind.

Had this woman been spending her days waiting by the phone for me to call? Had she spent her evenings trembling in fear at the silent void this building became each night?

No doubt the answer was yes. Nothing had changed, after all, and I thought of how heavily the building's silence had weighed on myself too.

But in recent days I had forgotten all about the stillness of the building. My sole preoccupation now was the first long-term job I had landed since my divorce.

Why? What had made the difference?

The answer had to be Asakusa. That night's events had completely transformed my state of mind. That remarkable couple had lifted me free of the dark solitude in which I had become so helplessly mired.

Yet here I am, scarcely five days later, claiming those events feel like ancient history? What has gotten into me?

I felt like a bad son—a wayward son who neglected his parents and pursued only his own selfish interests. I reproached myself.

What did it amount to, anyway, this life I led? Busying myself with random tasks that popped up one after another, enjoying the moments of excitement each little stir brought before it receded into the distance, yet accumulating no lasting store of wisdom from any of it. Each new day went by in much the same way. I never attained maturity, while I found myself growing ever more feeble with age.

How could I have pushed that extraordinary evening so far out of my mind in such a few short days—as if it had been nothing at all?

A man and a woman who looked astonishingly like my dead father and mother had welcomed me into their home, comforted me, rejoiced with me, and treated me with the kindness and affection one can expect only from one's parents.

How much of that experience had been a figment of my imagination? Wasn't that the first thing any normal person would want to know?

I must be made of water and indifference, I thought. An irrepressible desire to rush back to Asakusa and knock on the couple's door surged through me.

But I cooled my feverish impulse. I strove very hard to cool my impulse. You capricious, mindless hack, you, I chided myself. It's much too late to go to Asakusa tonight.

What time do you think it is, anyway? There was something miraculous in what you experienced that night. You can't go racing back on a whim and expect to find answers about things like that.

More pressing at the moment was the question of what to do about the call from the woman on the third floor.

I had in fact invited her. I had said she should come by for drinks. Or maybe it was only to chat.

I picked up the phone but immediately realized I didn't know her number. I reached for the directory and began searching for a Fujino listed at this address. The full name was given as Katsura Fujino. A name like that could be a man's, too, but I assumed it was the woman's own.

She answered on the second ring.

"Hello. Fujino," she answered crisply.

"This is Harada on the seventh floor," I said.

"Oh, hello."

"I'm sorry to be calling so late."

"Drinks?"

"Can you?"

"It's Friday."

She would be up in ten minutes, no, five, she said, without the slightest shade of gloom in her voice. It was hardly the tone of a person who trembled in fear of the night.

Since I had thought I'd be extending a hand of comfort to a woman weary with loneliness, her apparent good cheer caught me a little by surprise, but I quickly realized that was better than to have her show up in a funereal mood. That's right, I nodded to myself. It's Friday. I easily lost track which day of the week it was when no series of my own was airing.

"Kei," the woman said when I asked what I should call her. She dropped onto the sofa and began pulling the lid from a plastic container she'd brought with her. Inside were a knife and several small chunks of cheese.

"Officially, in my family register, it's Katsura. But since *fuji* and *katsura* are both trees, doesn't putting them together conjure some strange grafting experiment? So I decided to use the Chinese reading for *katsura* and go by Kei instead. Or you can think of it just as the letter K, or as the English name Kay—whatever you like."

"That's quite an assortment of cheeses you've got there."

"I've been slivering away at them, so they're all getting pretty small."

"Maybe I'll take this one with the dark mold on it."

"Are you sure?" She seemed amused.

"Is it that bad?"

"Most people go *bleaghh*."

"In that case, you better just give me a tiny little slice."

"Actually, I use these cheeses as a kind of character test. Which one you choose tells me what kind of person you are."

"So what does a slice of the moldy stuff tell you?"

"You're young at heart."

"You needed the cheese to tell you that?"

"Well, in your case, you look young, too, but sometimes I run across teenagers who refuse to eat anything but processed Snow Brand."

"You can't very well call them old just for that."

60

"But they *are* old, people like that."

"One shochu on the rocks," I said, setting her drink in front of her.

"One slice of cheese marbled with mold," she said, pushing a small plate across the table.

We both laughed and took a sip of our drinks. I had poured a brandy for myself. She had specifically requested the shochu vodka.

She was full of bright cheer. She wore a yellow T-shirt and blue jeans. Yet, something about the way she carried her softly rounded, mid-thirtyish figure seemed vaguely out of keeping with her spirited banter and good humor.

"Did you realize you walked right past me in the lobby day-before-yesterday morning?" she asked. "I didn't think so. You came out of the elevator with a frightfully intense look on your face and headed straight for the door without so much as a glance in my direction. What are you thinking about at times like that? . . . Oh, really? What kind of show— like a murder mystery or something? . . . Oh, so it's about sports. Come to think of it, I've seen a lot of athletes wearing that same look you had."

There was something artificial about her cheerfulness.

Perhaps she made it a point of pride not to display her depression—though, since she had originally shown up at my door drunk and pleading loneliness, it seemed a tad late to start hiding her melancholy now.

"Oh, well, I quit," she suddenly murmured in barely more than a whisper.

"Quit what?"

"It's too exhausting."

"Let me switch seats with you. That sofa can wear you out if you're not a sloucher."

"I swore to myself before I came that I'd keep my conversation light and gay."

"You don't need to impose a burden like that on yourself."

"I've unimposed it."

She smiled gently. For the first time her speech and her bearing seemed in harmony. "Even small talk takes so much work. Now that I'm past thirty, I need to lower my key an octave or so."

"Can I interest you in some brandy yet?"

"I still have some of this."

We both fell silent for a moment, and the sound of the busy traffic outside asserted itself.

"Shall I put on some music?"

"No, thanks," she smiled. "I listen to music a lot when I'm alone."

"I'm sorry, but I don't think I'm going to be able to finish even this small slice."

"You have to figure some people actually like the stuff, though, right? At least in other countries."

"Otherwise they wouldn't keep making it."

"I like acquiring new tastes. Even when I can't stand the taste at first, I keep trying, again and again, until at last I suddenly see what people think is so great about it. Then I feel like I've learned something new about Europeans."

"Sounds like you're a real grind."

"That's right. I can't just enjoy myself."

"But you do after all, don't you?"

"Yes, I suppose so. It just takes me some time."

Well, I hope you'll take your time with me, too, so you'll see one day what's great about me. The quip formed in my head, but I did not utter it aloud. I shied away from getting too deeply involved.

She was a remarkably beautiful woman. My first impression had been of a somewhat too broad forehead and thick lips, but studying her as we talked, I found that her eyes held a powerful allure. Several times I caught myself gazing only at those eyes. They made me pass over her defects.

"Don't you have an assistant or something?" she asked.

"Nope."

"You know how TV personalities come across like they actually live the way you see them on TV? Well, when I find out that those comedians who are always cutting up and making me laugh are actually part of a very serious business with lots of apprentices that they drive like slaves, I feel like I've been had somehow."

"I'm entirely alone," I said. "I suppose that calls for an explanation."

"Oh, no, I didn't mean to pry."

"You haven't said anything about why you're alone, either."

"I have an ugly burn." She said it without the slightest hesitation. "Right here," she said, putting her hand to her chest. "I've had some skin grafts, but it's still badly scarred and the colors don't quite match." She swallowed the last of her shochu. "It's not the sort of thing you want to talk about with your neighbors, but some of the people at my last apartment wouldn't leave me alone and kept badgering me about why I was still single. It got to be suffocating."

I searched for a response. "That actually gives me something good to say about this place for once," I finally said.

"Could I have some brandy?"

"Here, let me give you a fresh glass."

I poured.

"This sorry place drove everyone else away and made it possible for us to meet," I reprised. "You know, that was refreshing—the way you spoke right up about yourself. In fact, I've been admiring your forthrightness ever since you first came to my door. It's not often that a man within arm's reach of fifty can spend such a relaxing evening with a beautiful young woman like you."

"And to top it off, you now know that the woman has a handicap, so why hold back at all, right?"

"That's not what I meant. I didn't mean it sexually."

"I wish you did mean it sexually. There's nothing to keep me from having a good time so long as the room is dark. And my back is perfectly normal, so it'd be okay even in the light if you came from behind."

For a moment or two, she did not move. I *couldn't* move. Then she placed her brandy glass back on the table carefully so as not to make a sound.

I was once again left searching for words.

"It happens every time," she said quietly. "I make a mess of it. Do you mind if I get a glass of water?" She started to get to her feet.

"I'll get it," I said, hopping up for the kitchen sink.

The woman settled back into her seat, her two hands resting on her knees.

"Here you are. Shall I get you some ice?"

"No, this is fine."

She took a sip.

"Perhaps I'd better be going."

"Please stay. Let's drink a little more, get a little drunk."

"I couldn't stand getting drunk now. That'd be the worst," she said.

"Oh, but why not? It wouldn't be the worst, and besides, you haven't made a mess of it. I think it's lovely to hear a person speaking straight from the heart like that."

In truth, her words had carried no suggestion of wantonness to me. Rather, they had genuinely touched me—though I hesitated to say so for fear of sounding insincere.

"Then will you kiss me?" she asked. Her eyes remained averted.

"Of course," I hurried to say lest there be any more awkwardness. But if I kissed her now, it would come off as an act of charity. First I needed to put myself on an equal footing.

"I think you're beautiful."

"You only say that because you haven't seen."

She slumped forward as though her strength had suddenly left her.

I slid onto the sofa beside her and touched her shoulder.

"No, really. I think you're beautiful," I said again.

"Please don't."

To praise her beauty was perhaps to rebuke her hidden ugliness. But no other words had come to mind.

Don't be a fool! I scolded myself. At times like this, a woman doesn't want words. Right? Besides, the true meaning of a kiss has a way of making itself known, one way or another . . .

My lips were pressed to hers. It was a long, lingering kiss—a kiss that seemed a prelude to the act of love.

But when I put my hand to her breast, she squirmed free and turned her back to me.

"The burn isn't your fault," I said.

It was a silly thing to say. I had never faced anything like this before during an intimate encounter.

"I'd like to use your bathroom," she said in a low voice. "I need to borrow a towel to cover my chest."

She rose to her feet and disappeared into the bathroom.

It seemed like much ado about nothing. No matter what the nature of her keloids, no matter how ugly the aftermath of her skin grafts, I could not imagine being bothered by them. In fact, knowing she'd been through hardship filled me with sweet tenderness.

I should just look at her chest and get it over with, I thought. She was being unreasonable. Why should she insist that I come at her from behind? I wouldn't have it.

I heard water splashing in the shower.

If I barged in on her now it would terrorize her. I certainly didn't want to force the issue that way. No, I would find a chance to quietly uncover her scarred chest, and then reassure her that it didn't matter to me one whit. That was where we needed to start.

But when she reappeared naked before me except for a

blue towel clutched to her chest, her eyes drilled sharply into mine.

"You have to promise," she demanded. "I know you can easily pull this towel away any time you want, but you have to promise not to."

"I know it won't bother me," I told her, "no matter what kind of scars you have. It won't change how I feel about you."

"No," she said. "You mustn't see."

She refused to budge. I could tell from the steel in her voice that she would not come one step closer until I had made my pledge.

"Well, if it means that much to you," I nodded in assent.

"Promise?"

"I promise."

Still she did not move. "You might think I'm blowing things all out of proportion," she said, "but this is like those stories in the ancient myths. The woman tells the man he mustn't look, but he does anyway, and nothing can undo the damage it causes between them."

"Not in the ancient myths," I said, "but there're other stories, too."

"Like?"

"A young girl is convinced that she's hopelessly ugly. In the eyes of others, she's beautiful in so many different ways, but she wants to kill herself because, say, she thinks her legs are fat. Or a pimple is taking forever to go away, so she thinks there's no point in going on living."

For several moments Kei stood looking at the floor

67

without moving. Was she angry? Did she regret taking a shower now that she knew she couldn't trust me?

When she finally raised her head again, there was a distinct shade of weariness in her eyes.

"You're making fun of me."

"You're right. That was out of line."

"Promise me you won't look. No matter what."

"I won't look, no matter what. I promise."

She slowly came toward me.

The whiteness of her shoulders filled my vision as she approached, and a mild sense of intoxication swept over me.

Now she was before me. Droplets of water glistened on her broad forehead.

As I took her in my arms, she deftly spun around to turn her back to me.

On the rich whiteness of her left shoulder, I discovered a small dark mole.

"You have a pretty mole," I said, touching it with my finger.

"On my waist and hip, too," she said. Shaking her hair as if to loosen her tightly stretched nerves, she let out a barely audible giggle.

"You're right. The one on your waist is pretty, too."

It was as if a tiny splatter of India ink had fallen on that spot, leaving the skin as perfectly smooth as it had always been.

I dropped to my knees.

"And so is the one on your hip."

Gently stroking the white, well-rounded cheeks of her buttocks with my fingertips, I began by pressing my lips to the tiny black mole on her leftward rump.

6

The next two days I spent working on my proposal. On the third day, I set out for Asakusa. The time was shortly after noon.

My interlude with Kei had dissolved the impulse that had gripped me so powerfully that evening—the urge to rush headlong out the door for Asakusa. Just as my night in Asakusa had eclipsed my earlier concerns about Kei's state of mind, so this new turn in my relationship with Kei had pushed aside Asakusa.

But I could not simply forget those events and move on. Deep within me resonated still the tenderness in the couple's voices as they urged me, "Don't be a stranger, now," and, "Yes, do come again." Although I no longer craved the kind of emotional comfort I had found in their presence, I did know the night had a way of playing tricks on a person's perceptions, and I longed to ascertain just how much of my extraordinary encounter with them might have been a product of the nocturnal hour. This was why I set out in the middle of the blazing summer day: I needed to look reality in the eye under the all-illuminating light of the sun.

To a degree, too, my timing was motivated by a measure of fear—the fear of meeting that couple another time under the veil of darkness. After all, the likeness they bore to the mother and father I'd carried in my mind's eye for the past thirty-six years was truly beyond belief. Of course, images engraved in memory at the age of twelve could not, by themselves, provide a reliable impression of their every feature. And yet, somehow, the amazing sense of tranquility that enfolded me while I was with them had all but convinced me that they were indeed my parents.

Among the fondest memories from my childhood was that of coming home from a long, hard-marching school excursion, throwing down the school bag my mother had made for me out of an old Imperial Army haversack, casting off my shirt and pants and socks, flopping down on the tatami in my underwear, and, utterly free of the need to keep up appearances or my guard, drifting drowsily off to sleep as my mother went about her preparations for dinner in the kitchen. Something closely akin to the wonderful sense of security I'd felt at such times as a child had descended on me that night in Asakusa.

I could recall no such moments in all the years since my parents had died. Of course, at one time I had enjoyed many hours of relaxation and refuge from worldly cares with my former wife, but the sense of complete security I had experienced as a child was something else.

Perhaps a certain stiffness on my part, from feeling that a man should not presume too much upon a woman's solicitude, had frustrated my wife's protective impulses. I believed that a woman's maternal instincts were meant to be exercised solely upon her children, and that for a man to seek such qualities from his wife was to twist the relationship between them into something it ought not be. Over the years, I had often heard people say things like "He can't do anything for himself, I have to do everything for him" or "I won her over by appealing to the mother in her." But as for myself, I found it impossible to fall wholeheartedly into my wife's maternal embrace and let her dote on me.

As I see it now, the perpetual stress I had been under since the age of twelve had rendered me woefully inept at accepting the goodwill of others. Those who go through healthy childhoods learn that exhibiting a suitable degree of dependence is how one gains others' love. But an unfortunate adolescence had deprived me of this secret, and the deficiency had gradually placed a chill on my relationship with my wife.

I could tell that my wife found the lack of warmth in our relationship increasingly difficult to bear. Yet she refused to broach the subject of divorce, and I ultimately realized I had to be the one to break the ice. This, at any rate, was the position I took during the proceedings. For her part, my wife continued throughout to insist that she had never stopped loving me—though now, it seemed, she had already fallen into bed with Mamiya. Well, that was fine. That was all very well and good. The important point was that, in the final analysis, even in divorce, I had been denied the passive role. I had had to take the initiative myself, I had had to bear the blame myself, and, although the amount itself was in no way unreasonable, I had also had to give up the better part of our assets, including the house we had made our home and the land it stood on.

The entire experience had taken its toll on me and left me emotionally spent.

I longed to return to a passive role—to the carefree joy of simply doing as my mother and father said.

"Here, spread this hand-towel over your lap. In case you spill something."

"See. You hardly got the words out of your mouth before you dropped one."

Perhaps somewhere deep in my heart I had been yearning precisely for the tranquility such words could bring.

And my desire had crystallized into a single night's illusion. It had all seemed much too real for an illusion, but I found it easier to accept that a temporary emotional disturbance had been responsible for it than to come up with another explanation. Of course it did not feel particularly good to have to admit to a mental weakness capable of triggering such a disturbance, but it seemed the most plausible way to account for my experience that night.

This time I got off the subway at Tawara-machi station instead of going all the way to the end of the line at Asakusa.

I recalled how I'd once taken offense when I heard a TV news anchor misread the name as Tawara-*cho*, using the other common reading for the final character. I felt like he had slighted my hometown. It's Tawara-*machi*, you idiot, I'd snarled at the TV. Even though I hardly ever came back to visit anymore, a measure of loyalty still lingered in my veins.

Now back in that old district of mine, I climbed the stairs from the subway and emerged onto the sidewalk. The fiery, midsummer sun beat down relentlessly upon the shabby, discolored townscape. I was on my way to meet that remarkable couple again, and yet, because of the nagging doubts I carried with me, the sun struck me as relentless and the townscape as shabby. My feet grew heavy.

The sense that I had come on a misguided quest grew stronger with each step I took. I knew that the events I remembered could hardly have been real, so I also knew pretty well that coming back here to learn the truth, whatever it might be, could lead only to disillusionment. Why, then, was I making my way to the one place where all the sweet memories of that evening were most certain to be shattered?

I had bought some cookies and a bottle of saké in Jiyugaoka on the way. I felt their weight in the grocery bag at my side.

That's right, I reminded myself. Since they shared their food and drink with me, it's only fitting that I bring them something in return. And besides, they probably won't be home in the middle of the day anyway. I'll just leave the gifts with their next-door neighbor or someone.

I easily found the alley where I needed to turn. I was not yet drunk when the man led me there, so I remembered the surroundings well.

A metal staircase scaled up the side of the building, exactly as I remembered. Following the man's example from the other time, I tried to create as little noise as possible as I walked up the stairs.

On my way here, the idea—I could not say whether it was more a fear or a hope—that the apartment might have disappeared, that I might not be able to find it again no matter how hard I tried, had become entwined with my anticipation. But the second-floor walkway on which I now stood appeared every bit as real as it had seemed before, and I could see the last door at the back where the couple lived standing wide open.

A blue plastic garbage pail sat against the door—presumably to keep the door from swinging shut. Since they could not be expecting me, I knew the door had not been propped open for my benefit. It was probably so they could get a cross breeze.

In spite of my attempt to silence my footsteps, I knew that the sound of my shoes on the metal stairs must have carried at least a little to every apartment in the building. If I stood at the top of the stairs for too long, the residents might start wondering. Striding briskly along the walkway as though suddenly pushed from behind, I stopped at the last apartment and knocked on the open door.

"Hello?" I called out, turning to look into the apartment with considerable trepidation.

"Oh, you came."

It was my mother. Or rather, it was the woman who looked in every discernible way like my mother when she was young. Kneeling at a low table in the middle of the tatami, she was turning a crank attached to some kind of plastic container.

"I'm sorry to drop in unannounced like this."

"Oh, never mind that. We don't have a phone, so everyone comes unannounced."

She went on turning the crank.

"It certainly is hot, isn't it?" she said. "Day after day."

"Yes, it certainly is."

I didn't recognize the device she was cranking.

74

"What is that?" I asked as I stepped out of my shoes and up into the apartment. People often chided me for holding back, but here, for some reason, I found myself walking right in without even asking, as if it were my own home and it was the most natural thing for me to do.

"I'm making ice cream."

"Oh."

"Honeybunch says the ready-made kind they sell in stores is too sweet."

"I've never seen one of those gadgets before."

"They're advertised on TV."

She couldn't possibly be my mother. Ice-cream makers like hers didn't exist in 1950 or 1951. There could be no question that this woman belonged to the present.

"Take off your pants and make yourself comfortable," she said.

"Excuse me?" I was startled by her suggestion.

"You don't want your pants to get wrinkled."

"Oh, that's quite all right."

Here I was, visiting some very recent acquaintances, and I'd come at a time when the wife was alone. I couldn't very well take my pants off.

"Then at least take your shirt off."

"I don't think I'd care to do that either."

"Why not?"

"I'd be down to my undershirt."

"Oh, go on. Putting on such airs!"

"It's not that, but . . ."

"Keep this going for me a minute, will you?"

75

"Huh?"

"Here, you just turn it like this, see. And again. And again."

The next thing I knew, I was turning the crank on the ice-cream maker in her place.

"I'll get you a nice cool washcloth."

She took a neatly folded washcloth from a cardboard box sitting against the wall and went to the kitchen sink.

"Oh," I remembered. "I brought you some cookies and a bottle of saké in that bag there."

"Why, thank you. You didn't have to do that."

"Yes, I know, but I ate and drank an awful lot the other night, so . . ."

"We had a merry old time, didn't we?"

"We sure did. So, where's Dad?"

The word slid naturally off my tongue. Referring to a married man without children as "Dad" seemed a little bit odd, but the woman didn't bat an eye.

"He's on the early shift today. He gets off around seven, so I suppose he'll be back around eight."

"Home at eight on the early shift?"

"That's what happens when you work at a place that stays open until two in the morning."

As she said this, she came at my face with the washcloth she had dampened. I instinctively pulled away.

"Sit still," she commanded, as if scolding a child.

I let her wipe my face as I continued turning the crank. She wiped around my neck as well.

"That must mean he doesn't get home until three sometimes."

"Is it getting harder yet?"

"Excuse me?"

"The cranking."

"Oh. Not yet."

"Then you don't need to be cranking so hard."

"Where exactly does he work?"

"It's a place in Shintomicho."

"That's quite a ways."

"He worked right here in Asakusa until not so long ago, but he never lasts, you know. He gets tired of the place, or something rubs him the wrong way, and he's out of there."

"I see."

"He's really good at his job, you know. He never wastes toppings or rice, and his sushi comes out perfect every time, and he always keeps his work area clean. Plus he's reasonably good-looking, isn't he? He has a way with the customers. He doesn't act like a know-it-all either, so his employers all love him."

"Uh-huh."

The woman went back to the sink to rinse out the washcloth. "But he doesn't know how to stay put. After a while he just ups and quits."

"I see."

I had idealized my father in my mind, so I felt a little taken aback to learn of this defect in his character. Except she's not actually talking about my father, I reminded myself. She's talking about her husband. I needed to stop confusing the two.

"There are so many sushi shops, you know," she went on. "If you're in the chef's association, you can go out and find a new job pretty much any time you want. That's what makes him so cocky. He can't stand chefs that talk like sushi's more important than life itself, so he won't have anything to do with the fancier shops."

"Well, just as long as he can keep food on the table, I suppose."

"We manage to eat, but an apartment like this is about the best we can ever hope for. Not that I'm complaining. There's no end to it if you start wishing you had more. So long as we can go on living together like this in our happy-go-lucky way, that's pretty much all I ask for."

"Mmm."

"Can I get you some beer?"

"No thanks."

It would hardly be proper to start drinking when I'd barged in in the middle of the day and the master of the house was away.

"Oh, there you go again, always trying to be so polite. It was the same the other night. You kept saying no thanks, I've had enough, thanks, but then you went right on drinking everything we offered you."

She was uncapping a bottle of beer even as she spoke. It seemed I would be having a drink after all.

As I felt the first flush of intoxication warming my body, I began to think there really wasn't anything so extraordinary about what had taken place.

I had simply run into a rather gregarious fellow who chose to invite me back to his apartment. His wife was also an easygoing person, and the three of us got drunk together, after which I went home. For some people, things like that happened all the time. Out of sentimentality, I had superimposed memories of my parents on the man and his wife. If I removed my personal projections from the picture, nothing so unusual had taken place that I needed to come all the way to Asakusa to find out "the truth."

The woman wore a trim, sleeveless dress with pale pink stripes, and I could see the marks of fresh mosquito bites on both of her arms. If this were really my dead mother, how could she appear before me looking so palpably alive, skin blemishes and all? And besides, if the man were in fact my dead father, he surely wouldn't stick it out until the end of his shift in Shintomicho when I had come to visit. I could not but conclude that I had a fragile temperament that easily let wild fancies carry me away.

"I had such a good time the other night," I said. "I just had to come by again to thank you."

"We actually thought we might see you back here a little sooner."

She poured some more beer into my glass. I glanced up at her profile as she tilted the bottle, and my heart went thump again. She did look so much like my mother.

I was struck also by how odd it seemed to be alone with a woman in her mid-thirties and not feel the slightest hint of sexual tension in the air. But then I realized it wasn't odd at all. When a woman looked so much like one's mother, it was only natural that sexual impulses would be suppressed.

But suppose her husband came home and discovered us like this. Then what? Would he buy it when I told him his wife looked so much like my mother that no improper thoughts ever entered my mind? Not very likely. I needed to leave. Lingering on over beer was definitely not a good idea. I didn't want to be a cause for unnecessary friction between such a nice couple.

I was on the verge of saying I'd better be going, when I swallowed my words. If I took my leave now, I would be left with the same doubts as before. Part of me still found it difficult to believe that the uncanny resemblance between this couple and my parents was purely accidental.

I had come all this way. I should at least ask her one thing—one of the questions that had led me to revisit this place.

"Shall I slice up some cucumbers or something for you to nibble on?" she asked.

"Thanks, but I'm afraid I need to be getting on my way."

"Already?"

"Yes, I need to be going."

"But you just got here."

"I'm sorry. I have a meeting. I'll come again. Please say hello for me."

"You really have to go so soon?"

"Unfortunately, yes . . ."

"Some TV station, I suppose?"

"That's right, in Akasaka."

"And here I was thinking we could all have dinner together."

"I really only came to deliver a token of my gratitude for the other night. Instead, I'm drinking your beer again."

"Oh, stop acting like such a stranger."

I bowed with deliberate formality and got to my feet.

"Dad will be disappointed," she said.

"I'll come again."

I knew it was time for that question, but I still shrank from voicing it aloud.

"They were forecasting a typhoon to come our way, but it looks like maybe it's fizzled out."

She spoke to my back as I put on my shoes at the door. Her voice, too, was indistinguishable from my mother's.

I knew I could not let the opportunity pass. "You may think this is a strange thing for me to ask after all this time, but . . ."

"What?"

"I don't know your name. I mean, since you don't display a name plate by your door."

"My word! What're you talking about? It's Harada, of course." The woman spoke my surname without a trace of self-consciousness, then burst out laughing. "This heat must have really gotten to your head. What child asks his own parents their name?"

For a fraction of a second I felt helpless under the massive sledgehammer that was poised to come crashing down on my skull. Then the sledgehammer dealt me its blow.

"I guess you're right. Ha ha ha. It must be the heat." I managed to recover my breath just enough to force the words out. I could not turn to face her.

"See you then," I said, bowing.

"We'll be expecting you."

"Uh-huh."

"Take care now."

"Good-bye."

I tried with all my might to maintain a normal gait as I moved away from the door, but the wave of terror was swelling up rapidly. As I started down the metal staircase, my feet gathered speed with each step, and by the time I came out of the alley onto the shopping street I had broken into a full run. Every organ in my body seemed to erupt in a frenzy of horror.

God! Oh, God! I cried silently. I was not religious, but at that moment I desperately wanted to call upon any god that might be listening.

I hailed a cab, but when it pulled up I waved it on.

"Never mind. I'm sorry."

The thought of being enclosed in a small compartment with no one else but the driver had sent a shudder of terror through me. What if the driver turned to look at me and his face was my father's?

"You've been watching too many old horror films," I chided myself. When I noticed people giving me strange looks I realized I had said the words aloud.

I glanced anxiously over my shoulder as I hurried toward the Tawara-machi subway station, terrified that I might see my mother coming after me.

To my great relief, she was not.

7

That evening, a violent thunderstorm passed over the city.

I watched the driving rain and lightning from a bar on the top floor of a high-rise hotel. The rain dashed against the glass in torrents, making the window a blur. It turned the jagged bolts of lightning stabbing at the earth into nothing more than diffuse flickers, which irritated me a little. I ached to smash the massive pane and see the lightning bolts descend in all their piercing brilliance. I longed to distance myself from anything ambiguous, anything non-transparent, anything belonging to darkness. I wanted to be in a world where all was bright and clean and in sharp focus. Precisely for that reason, I had steered clear of basement and ground-level establishments to seek out brighter environs, high in the sky, but thanks to thunderclouds, abetted by the gathering dusk, the realm of darkness had encroached moment by moment upon my world even here.

I dreaded going home and having to face my empty apartment alone. Not that I had anything to fear from the apartment itself, of course. What I needed to fear was my own self. I knew that perfectly well.

I remained at an utter loss how to explain the hallucinations I was having, of my long-dead parents suddenly reappearing before me in exactly the image I had of them when they died.

Not for the most fleeting of moments had my visit today seemed like a hallucination. My mother had appeared before me as a discrete other, as vivid and physically real as the whiskey glass into which I now gazed. How could I believe that she had been purely a figment of my imagination? She had even served me beer, from which a warm and pleasant feeling of intoxication had lingered in my body until only a short time ago.

Yet, none of it could possibly have been real. I had to have imagined the whole thing.

And what was more, it seemed I lacked the ability or power to free myself of these hallucinations—to heal myself of whatever might be causing them. A feeling of helplessness gnawed at the pit of my stomach. I did not doubt that losing my parents at the tender age of twelve had left me with certain emotional scars. But I knew that even those who reached adulthood with both parents intact bore childhood wounds of one kind or another, so I had always figured I was pretty much the same as everyone else in having old baggage to contend with. The difference, to my mind, was in how well a person controlled and tamed the unfortunate legacies of his birth and childhood as he proceeded on through his adult life, and for my own part, I believed that I had long since resolved such matters and put them behind me. Never had I anticipated that they might suddenly rear their heads in this form.

I could only suppose that these hallucinations manifested a subconscious hunger for something that had been left unfulfilled because I lost my parents at such a young age. On a conscious level, certainly, I had considered myself to be mostly free of such desires, yet when I thought of the soothing sense of security I felt in the couple's presence, I could conclude but one thing: somewhere deep inside of me I had been yearning desperately for the warm embrace of parental love. It would reasonably follow, then, that this hidden yearning had risen to the surface in the form of hallucinations in the days of solitude following my divorce. Yet, truth be told, I had great difficulty accepting this as a satisfactory explanation of what I had experienced.

Could a hallucination really feel so vividly real? If my imagination had made up the events in Asakusa today, then this bar, this entire hotel, and even the thunder and lightning and rain outside this window, had to be its product as well. I was as certain of my mother's presence with me in that apartment this afternoon as I was of the people and furnishings surrounding me in this bar now—and the same was true for my father the other night. There could be no denying the palpable reality.

Whatever the truth of the matter, I needed to deal with it calmly.

I didn't want to believe it possible, but I feared this experience might portend an impending nervous collapse—a breakdown triggered by a deep-seated weakness in me. If so, I had to find some way to forestall it.

The last thing I needed right now was another drink, I realized. What I did need was to go on home and get back to work. My best chance for fighting off these hallucinations could well be in sticking to my normal routine and refusing to let it be disrupted.

I caught a cab back to my apartment. By the time we pulled up at the entrance, the storm had passed. A brilliant moon shone down on the nearly empty parking lot.

As I rode up in the elevator I decided my first act would be to turn on every light in the apartment—not only the overheads, but the ones on my desk, on my bed stand, and in the bathroom. Somehow I needed to drive off the terror that had followed me all the way from Asakusa. I still cringed recalling the words: "What child asks his own parents their name?"

I opened the door to the dark apartment and flicked the switch for the living-room light. The bedroom light came next, then the small lamp on my nightstand and my desk lamp and the light in the toilet.

Then I froze in panic.

The light in the bath compartment failed to come on. I flicked the switch back and forth several more times, but darkness persisted. Suddenly I sensed an eerie presence lurking there. Terror gripped me as I awaited the grotesque hand that would come reaching slowly up out of the tub, followed by an arm, then a face, and then at last the full figure of a ghoulish monster standing there glaring at me.

My mouth wide open, gasping for breath, I slammed the door shut. It was all I could do to keep from screaming.

Stop being ridiculous! It's only a burnt-out light bulb. That's all. Why should I be standing here quaking in fear?

But even as I tried to reassure myself, I remained petrified with fright. Petrified, but hearing something. The sound of . . . what could it be? Oh, it's the intercom. The chime on the intercom. Nothing strange about that. Someone's at the door pushing my doorbell. Nothing wrong with that. But who? Suppose it's my father. Or my mother.

I went to answer. I realized I was letting wave after wave of terror wash over me as I flailed helplessly about, and I hated myself for it. "Get a hold of yourself!" I hissed, and lifted the handset.

"Hi. It's me," Kei said.

I couldn't have been more relieved.

I opened the door and found her standing there in a pale green blouse and yellow skirt.

"Can I come in?" she asked, tilting her head a little to one side.

I chose not to tell Kei about the day's events.

I really wasn't sure what people normally did at times like this. I wondered if maybe I was being paranoid, and several times I almost started to confide in her, but each time I found myself holding back.

It wasn't as if I'd been accosted and mugged on the street. The hallucinations I had experienced might owe to a personal infirmity, and I did not want Kei to see me cowering in fear before something I could not understand.

"I saw you from the window when you came inside a while ago," she said. "You looked so pale and worn out, I was worried."

"It's probably only because the moon was so bright," I said, making light of her worries. "I don't feel the least bit tired." She was thirty-three, and as a man fifteen years her elder, I instinctively tried to conceal any signs of flagging vitality.

"Are you sure?" She was in my arms. "You didn't seem quite normal, somehow."

"Ooh," I squealed mockingly, "and was there some kind of ghostly aura hovering about me, too, maybe?" My tone was joking, but I had in fact taken her remark more than half seriously. The sharpness of a woman's intuition is legendary.

"Actually, yes," Kei said. "This may sound spooky, but it almost seemed like you were off in another dimension or something."

"Or maybe like I was an apparition?"

"Yes, like you were an apparition. And that's why I half expected not to find you home when I rang your doorbell."

"So, do you think I'm an apparition now?"

"Hardly. Not with a nose hair sticking out like that."

We both laughed and fell into a passionate embrace.

She insisted again that I must not touch or see her chest, so for a second time I began our act of love by wrapping my arms about her shapely, white buttocks with the lovely little mole on her leftward rump.

That evening I learned that Kei worked in the accounting department of a packinghouse, and that she'd been born and raised in a small farm village about an hour by bus from Toyama on the Sea of Japan coast.

The next day I spent from shortly after noon until nearly midnight observing what went on at a pool hall I'd visited once before for about an hour. The show was still waiting for the official green light, but the producer had asked me to go ahead and get started on the first episode because they might not have enough time for filming if I waited until the proposal had formally cleared all of the hurdles.

He was very confident of approval, saying it was a virtual lock unless one of the sponsors came up with something very particular to make a stink about. If the production company had been an outside contractor, I would nevertheless have waited for the official go-ahead before beginning, since it wasn't uncommon for TV stations to turn down what seemed like a sure thing in the final stage of negotiations. But in this case the series was being produced in-house by the station, and all of the relevant departments had already signed off on the project. My visit to the pool hall was my last chance to observe its habitués in action before picking up my pen.

I began writing the following morning.

A little after nine that evening, the phone rang. Kei said she'd gotten some eel bones to have with drinks and wondered if she could come up.

I'd filled fifty-three pages of 200-character manuscript paper on my first day of writing, and it had put me in a very good mood. We drank and talked until eleven and then parted with nothing more than kisses. I wanted to make love, but Kei said no.

"I don't want you to think I'm asking for sex every time I call," she said.

"I didn't think that," I said, but I knew at my age it would likely affect my ability to work the next day, so I was not inclined to press.

When we said good night, I kissed her once before opening

the door, and again after. Then I watched after her until the elevator doors slid shut behind her.

The next morning I rose at seven and got to my desk at eight. By evening I had filled sixty-eight more pages. That gave me a two-day total of 121 pages, which, depending on the nature of the show, could suffice for a full episode. But we were aiming at a show with particularly lively dialogue. The characters were supposed to be both loquacious and fast-spoken, and my instincts told me I needed another forty pages or so, even with a certain amount of time being eaten up by billiards and tennis action that had no dialogue.

Quite worn out by the effort, I went to a nearby Italian restaurant for dinner, then stopped at the video store to rent Eddie Murphy's latest on my way home. I poured myself some beer and started the tape, but soon fell fast asleep on the sofa. When I woke up in the middle of the night, I stumbled to my bed trying not to let my mind get going. Fortunately, I drifted quickly back to sleep. I had filled the entire day with work and routine activities, and managed to keep my parents at a distance.

On the third day I finished the episode. At 165 pages, I wondered if it might even be a little on the long side, but the script for the first episode of a series typically included extra staging directions about the characters as well as the locales and buildings where the action was set. Discounting for that, the net dialogue probably came to a little under 160 pages.

The work had progressed at a pace I seldom hoped to achieve. Sometimes I would spend an entire day struggling to turn out just three pages, and then, in the end, throw out even those the next morning. When this went on for more than a day or two, I wondered seriously whether it was time for a change of profession. For the moment, though, I was brimming with energy. The story was taking shape nicely. The characters had all sprung quickly to life and begun advancing along their separate paths toward the next episode.

And I was done at barely three in the afternoon. I still needed to read the draft over and make corrections, but that could wait until tomorrow. Letting the manuscript sit for a day would make it easier to spot any problems.

This meant I had some free time on my hands, and it seemed a shame to spend it all alone in my apartment. Unfortunately, Kei would still be at work, and I didn't know anyone else I could call at three in the afternoon and expect to join me.

At times like this in the past I used to ask my wife to go to the movies with me, but the exhilaration of a job successfully completed was, after all, only my own, and I soon realized that my wife did not really feel a part of it. I learned not to express my pleasure so overtly. I would need to be careful about such things with Kei as well.

For the first episode to have flowed so effortlessly from my pen boded well for the future of the series, so my delight encompassed more than just my latest accomplishment; it brought pleasure of a different kind from when the script for a one-shot special has an easy delivery. I felt quite confident that what I'd written would exceed the producer and the director's expectations. Although I had not been very excited about the series at first, once I actually sat down to write, I'd quickly made it my own. I had been able to steer the story and the characters in a direction that pleased my fancy.

I took the subway to Ginza and entered a beer hall. The mid-afternoon crowd was very sparse. As I sipped at a pint of lager, I gradually turned my thoughts toward my mother and father. I'd pushed them out of my mind over the last few days, but now I finally felt ready to take a very slow and deliberate look over my shoulder again.

When I did, I found my mother and father beaming back at me. Not that they actually stood there behind me in the beer hall, of course, but that I saw them watching warmly over me in my mind's eye.

"We'll be expecting you. Take care now," my mother said.

I had fled that encounter in horror, but when I stopped to think about it, neither she nor my father had ever done anything to hurt me. If I were to tell my mother how elated I was at finishing the script so quickly, I felt quite certain she would share my excitement.

What I had experienced in Asakusa could hardly be called normal, and there was even a high probability that it had all taken place entirely in my cranium. But as I reflected on those events now, I found myself asking whether there could be anything so terribly wrong with giving myself over to imaginary fancies from time to time.

Of course, if I were being tormented by frequent hallucinations even when I was at home and at work, then therapy would be in order—to banish the visions from my mind once and for all. But these were pleasant, heart-warming hallucin-ations that visited me only when I went to Asakusa, and they filled me with both comfort and strength. What need did I have to eschew them?

It was only from words spoken to my back that I'd learned the woman was my mother. We had not yet had a chance to speak as parent and child.

A mother and father in their thirties with a forty-eight-year-old son could not be of the real world, of course, but if an imagined world could allow such a relationship to exist, then I was ready to embrace that world. The terror I'd felt before was gone; floating before me were my parents' joyful smiles welcoming me into their home.

The joyful smiles of loved ones delighted to see me were not unknown to me—I had experienced them for a brief time with my wife, and also when my son was still a toddler—so I did not feel I had lived a particularly deprived life compared to others in this respect. That my yearning for my parents' smiling faces was nevertheless so powerful as to produce these hallucinations owed, I supposed, to the eternal child in me.

If I smothered this eternal child, then wouldn't I also be snuffing out the child's thirty-something parents who had returned to live anew in their beloved Asakusa? They were there for *me*, and though by all appearances they spent the days between my visits busy with their own work and play, it seemed quite possible that all time other than the time they spent with me was for them a void in which neither of them actually existed. I pictured my parents frozen in the middle of some activity, like figures in a wax museum. Wasn't I the only one who could breathe life into them?

Rising to my feet, I strode out into the bright afternoon sun and hailed a cab.

8

As I turned from the shop-lined street into the alley and began climbing the metal staircase as softly as I could, I felt a knot of terror forming in the pit of my stomach again. I halted my steps before reaching the top.

What exactly were those people in the end?

Were they some kind of shape-shifting foxes or badgers of which old legends tell?

In the year they died, my father was thirty-nine and my mother thirty-five. That same father and that same mother could not be living in this apartment building thirty-six years later without having aged a day.

Random and fickle as our reality may sometimes seem, there remain certain things that can be and certain others that cannot. For a man of forty-eight to lose sight of that difference surely pointed to a very serious breakdown of some kind. When I so eagerly chose to embrace the unreal and rush back here by cab, was I in effect saying that I didn't really care about my life anymore?

I certainly didn't think of it that way.

I'd just completed, with a rare intensity of focus, the first episode of a series. I knew the draft was not bad, and I had plenty of energy left over to rejoice in my success. To my mind, it was not a despair-driven flight from reality that had brought me back to this place.

Yet, I had little doubt that when I climbed to the top of these steps and proceeded along the outside walkway to the last apartment at the back, I would find my parents—or at least two people who acted it and bore an indistinguishable likeness to my parents. Their presence had seemed as real as real could be, and my time with them had been so unforgettably sweet that I had been powerless to resist their allure.

I knew I might be advancing step by step into an ever more terrifying realm, yet I could not see how reversing course now would let me preserve anything of value. A man of healthier mind would forgo these stairs. But what could I hope to gain by turning back in the name of safeguarding my wobbling psyche? I doubted that a particularly bright future awaited me in the life to which I would be returning.

I climbed the last few steps to the second floor.

My mother and father were now only a dozen or so paces away.

This recognition brought with it a ticklish self-consciousness, and my legs seemed to recoil a little with each step. What was it going to be like? I wondered—to actually meet and speak with them as my parents for the first time.

There was so much I wanted to tell them. There was so much I wanted them to know about the years since I was twelve—everything I'd experienced, felt, and been through.

"Hideo."

It was my father's voice, calling me from behind. I froze and could not immediately turn around.

"Whachya standin' there for?"

The voice quickly moved up on me, and then I felt a light

96

pat on my shoulder as my father slipped past on his way to the door. Without turning around he said, "Wanna play some catch?"

"Where?" I asked, but my father had already disappeared inside. I quickly followed.

As before, the door had been propped open to let a cross breeze through.

"Is there a place like that around here?" I asked from the doorway.

"Goodness! When did you come?" my mother beamed at me from the kitchen sink.

"He was standin' there spaced out on the walkway," my father said with a laugh. Seating himself on the knee-high window sill across the room, he pulled at the cellophane wrapper on a package of cigarettes. He had apparently just returned from buying them.

"Hi!" I said, sounding a little like a twelve-year-old even to myself.

"Come on in," my mother said.

"Come in, come in," my father said.

"Just once," I said as I took off my shoes, "we played catch in the plaza in front of the International Theater. Remember that, Dad?"

"We must've done it more than once."

"No, just once. That's why I remember it so well. I always wished we could do it again. But we never got the chance."

"Shall we go toss a few, then?"

"Why don't you?" my mother urged.

"Is there still a park around here these days?"

97

"We can just play in the street out front. It'll be fine."

"You really think so?"

"All the stores are closed anyway. The whole city's practically deserted until the seventeenth."

Oh, right, it's August—the month when half of Tokyo goes home to the country for the Bon festival to greet the returning spirits of the dead. It wasn't only because of the time of day that the beer hall had been so uncommonly quiet.

My father poked around in the bottom half of the futon closet and soon came up with two baseball gloves. Both were well worn, but I couldn't remember having seen either of them before.

"You've got some real vintage gloves there," I said.

"Come to think of it," he said, "I only used a rubber ball with you, didn't I?"

That's right, I remembered. He had owned a regulation baseball, but insisted it was too dangerous for little kids and refused to use it with me. I wanted so badly to play catch with him with that ball, but he'd always made excuses that he was too busy—until finally, just that once, he agreed to play with me, with a rubber ball. He was all wrapped up in the league he belonged to with his sushi-shop buddies, and he didn't put a high priority on playing catch with his son.

"We'll step out for a while, then," I said to my mother.

"Have a good time," she called after us as we headed back outside. Once we got to the shopping street, we realized right away that playing there was impossible. My father had been right about most of the shops being shuttered, and the traffic was considerably below normal as well, but that didn't mean it was so quiet we could stand in the middle of the street throwing a ball back and forth.

"Shoot!" he said. "Oh, well. Let's go on up this way then." He set off at a fast clip, and I followed.

I was smiling. As a child, I'd thought of my father as being tough in fights and always on top of things, but I now imagined that he'd actually been more of the happy-go-lucky character I was tagging along after—shooting off his mouth while assuming the best, then keeping his cool when it turned out he was wrong and swaggering off to find another way.

The discovery cheered me. And although I savored the discovery as a forty-eight-year-old, I found myself transformed into a twelve-year-old boy again the moment we came to the street in front of Honganji Temple and my father's first throw smacked into my glove.

A fine throw, with plenty of juice.

"You've got a good arm, Dad."

"Whadja expect?"

Pausing now and then to let a pedestrian or car go by, we tossed the ball back and forth for nearly an hour. I reveled in the feeling that the hard or soft pop of each catch was bringing back just a little more of my long lost father to me. Each time a passing car forced me to step aside, I observed with satisfaction that it was unmistakably a recent model. And I noted with equal satisfaction that my father, too, had to step aside with me as the car went by.

"Car coming, car coming."

"Okey-dokey."

Time after time we interrupted our game with an exchange

99

like this and stepped over to the tall fence surrounding the temple. I savored each and every instance.

"Maybe we'd better be packing it in," my father finally said. "Mom'll get on my case if you're missing too long."

Even remarks such as these were delightful. I was realizing that, in some ways, my parents were not at all like my twelve-year-old impressions of them. I could see the mannerisms of a dashing artisan in the way my father swung his arms and strutted along, and I found it quite endearing.

Back at the apartment, the table was set with a bowl of edamame beans and a plate of garnished tofu to nibble on, plus three beer glasses.

"I wish we could offer you a shower," my mother said.

"Yeah, right," my father retorted. "And where the blazes would you propose to put such a thing?" He stripped to the waist at the kitchen sink and began wiping himself down with a cold washcloth. Though somewhat pale, he had a firm, muscular physique.

When he was done, I stripped to my sleeveless undershirt at the sink and followed suit.

My father turned on the TV. The summer high-school baseball tournament was on.

Next to the TV, an electric fan swung its neck back and forth.

"You sit here, Hideo," my mother beckoned. I sat down between them at the low table and held out my glass as she poured me some beer.

"Are you on the late shift today, Dad?" I asked.

"Nah, I quit."

"That's right," my mother said. "He up and quit again."

"Give me a break, will you? Have I ever let you go hungry?"

"No, but . . ."

"It was ridiculous. The place had a counter plus five tables, and I was the only one who could turn out decent sushi. The master was supposed to be getting out of the hospital in September so they begged me to stick it out through August, you know, but I'd had enough. You gotta think of what you're doing to your customers in the meantime. I mean, there was no way I could fix all the orders myself, so the customers wound up with all kinds of shameless crap, and, of course, nobody was happy about it. Fortunately, customers these days are pretty meek and you don't get them throwing fits, but just because they don't throw a fit doesn't mean everything's hunky-dory."

"Fine, dear. There's no sense in spoiling Hideo's visit by harping on that now."

"You brought it up."

I was on cloud nine. My parents had not had a TV when they died. Things like beer and edamame and tofu were much harder to come by then than today. The electric fan was new as well.

I'm so happy for you, Mom. I'm really glad you can live like this now, Dad.

"Stop being so stingy with your beer," my father said. "The way you're sipping at it, you'd think it was whiskey."

"That's right," my mother added. "Drink up. We can afford it."

I downed the rest of my glass in a single draft and held it out for my mother to pour me some more.

Maybe I could buy them a shower. An air conditioner wouldn't be a bad idea either. And I could have beer hauled in by the case.

But I supposed it would all be in vain. Like on the set of a movie, no matter how normal and real everything appeared on set, I had to assume I was somewhere a long way from reality. I had to assume that the moment I departed, my parents would cease moving, grow colorless, and be robbed of the breath of life.

"The other day," my father was saying, "you told us you wrote stuff for a living."

"He writes scripts for television, dear," my mother broke in. "Isn't that something?"

"What's so great about it? If you ask me, most writers know less about how the world really works than just about anyone else. They're a bunch of hypocrites and cowards, and to put it straight, I don't like 'em much."

"What in the world are you saying, dear? To your own son?"

"I'm not talking about Hideo. I'm just saying that's the way most of 'em are, on the whole. Writers basically don't have much feeling for how the rest of us live."

Even as I delighted in my father, so many years my junior, spouting off with such cocky self-assurance, a feeling of despair began to creep into my consciousness. My father was saying exactly the kind of things I'd expect him to say, and how could I be sure I was not putting every word of it into his mouth myself?

After all, the mother and father who were with me now could not actually be my mother and father of thirty-six years ago; they had to be a product of my own mind, for my true mother and father who had died all those years ago could not truly be brought back no matter how hard I kicked and screamed. The sooner I put an end to this delusional pursuit of long lost emotional comforts the better off I'd be.

On the other hand, when I looked again at the two figures sitting before me without the slightest aura of falseness about them, I found myself asking: how could I ever think these people existed only in my imagination?

"Dad," I said, "let's shake hands."

"Shake hands?"

"And you too, Mom."

"You're not leaving already, are you, dear?"

"Stay for supper. No sense in rushing away."

How sad to think that these words, too, I could have placed in their mouths myself.

"Relax, I'm not leaving. I just want to shake hands."

"Put 'er there," my father thrust out his hand. I gripped it firmly, and I distinctly felt his hand gripping back. I was not merely gripping my own hand.

"Now it's my turn," my mother said, extending her hand. Although her skin felt a little rough in places, her hand was softer than my father's and noticeably smaller.

I tried to etch into my memory everything about the way her hand felt against mine. Could I be hallucinating even this sensation of living flesh? I did not think so.

"And one more thing, Dad," I said, seeking yet another

tangible sign—something that could not come from within myself. "You play flower cards, right?" I'd remembered how his buddies used to come by to play the game.

"Sure. Why?"

"You think you might have a deck in the house, Mom?"

"Of course. Though it's been an awfully long time since we played."

"I'd like to learn."

I didn't know the first thing about how to play. If my father could teach me a game I didn't know, and if I could still remember it when I got home, then I would know for sure that he wasn't a product of my own imagination.

"You claim to be a writer and you don't even know how to play flower cards?"

"I did get pretty deep into mah-jongg once."

"What game'll it be, then? C'mon C'mon?"

"It doesn't matter. Isn't there one called Eighty-Eight that's for three players?"

"So you *do* know."

"That's about the extent of my knowledge."

"Flower Rummy might be best," my mother suggested.

I had no idea what the differences might be. "That'll be fine," I said.

If my mother and father could teach me how to play the game, there could no longer be any doubt that they existed apart from me. I would know once and for all that I was not merely hallucinating, that they truly existed.

My mother went to get the cards and gave them to my father. He took them from their box and began shuffling deftly.

"Okay, now. You know that the cards are divided into months, right?"

"Months?"

"Good grief, you mean you don't even know that much? Here, let's get this out of the way."

He abruptly shoved the table we'd been drinking from to one side. One of the beer bottles started to teeter, but I caught it just in time and held it as my mother carefully moved the table farther out of the way.

"Now, about this Flower Rummy game your mom suggested," my father said, "it won't hurt you to know that it's also called Flower Dummy. That's because any moron can play it. Are you ready?"

Sitting on the tatami with one knee up and the other folded flat against the floor, my dashing father began teaching me the game, obviously very pleased with himself.

9

I arranged to meet the producer of my new series at a coffee shop in Shibuya the next evening. I arrived first, and I noticed him blanch when he came in and recognized me.

He quickly covered up by breaking into a broad smile as he came toward me, but I suspected right away that something was wrong. It seemed to have become a regular pattern with my recent jobs; I could always count on some kind of a glitch.

The script for the first episode had come very smoothly. Not only had the initial draft progressed at a rare pace, but I'd found very few corrections to make when I read through it. In fact, everything had gone a little too easily. Something nasty had to be lurking around the corner.

"You work fast," he said, wiping the perspiration from his face with the cold cloth the waitress brought when she came to take his order for a glass of iced milk.

"I guess I was in some kind of groove."

"Can't complain about that," he said, avoiding my eyes as he unzipped his slim leather briefcase and pulled out a large manila envelope.

"I should have asked you on the phone to be sure to bring your personal seal with you."

"Why?"

"The station's new policy says we have to get all the paperwork in order before we accept any manuscripts," he said, drawing a document from the envelope. It was a contract between the station and me.

"It's a standard contract," he said. "Identical except for the amount entered as your scriptwriting fee. You'll need to affix your seal in three places. I've circled each spot lightly with a pencil."

"So this means we have the green light?"

"You got it. The sponsors all gave thumbs up. It's set to air beginning the second week of October, and the first episode will run as a special. I went down to Osaka yesterday to meet with R Pharmaceuticals, and when I got back I went straight from Tokyo Station to a five o'clock meeting at M. Cosmetics. This morning it was K. Automotive at ten. Man, oh, man! It's not the sort of legwork a producer ought to have to do. Someone on the marketing staff could tell them everything they need to know, but they all insist on hearing it from the producer. I tell you, I'm beat. Sorry I kept you in suspense so long. We're going to be on a tight schedule, with shooting to begin on location the first week of September. So we'll all appreciate whatever you can do to move things along."

"Here's the first episode," I said, handing him my manuscript.

"Thanks. I'll read it right away and call if I have any questions."

"Sure."

The waitress came back with the glass of iced milk.

So it appeared there had been no snags after all, at least for the time being.

Or was that what he was going to hit me with next?

It turns out the lead actress is three months pregnant, and she doesn't know who the father is. But she insists she wants to have the baby. With shooting lasting three months, she'll be six months pregnant by the end, and it's obviously going to show. Of course, most of the time we can do creative things with her wardrobe to hide it, but I'm afraid we'll have to avoid scenes where she plays tennis. We're also a little worried how the public will react to having an unwed mother in the role. It'll be all to the good if they're sympathetic, but hey, it could just as easily go the other way. Finding a replacement at this stage could be tough, but if that's what it's going to be, we need to move fast.

No doubt it would be something like that. I knew I was letting my imagination get away from me, but better to be prepared for the worst. That way it would come as less of a blow.

"Oh," he said, as though suddenly remembering something.

Here it comes, I thought.

"Is there anything I need to know beforehand about the first episode?"

"I think we covered the bases when we did the research together."

"Good."

"Just read the script."

"You sound like you're pretty pleased with it."

I sensed that he wanted to say something more. His eyes shifted about, and he seemed to have something on his mind.

"You're acting like you have something else to tell me," I said, with a nervous smile.

"Huh?"

"Something's come up, hasn't it?"

"Why would you think that?"

"The look on your face when you came in wasn't what I'd call A-OK."

More precisely, it was the look on his face when he came in and caught sight of me. That's right, I recalled. It was when he saw *me* that his expression had changed.

"You might think it's none of my business," he said with a nervous laugh.

"What?"

"And you might get mad at me for fretting about nothing, but—"

"Is this about me?"

"—you *are* in good health, aren't you?"

"Why do you ask?"

"Well, you know, producers are that way. They're always walking on pins and needles, wondering what might go wrong."

"So far as I know, I'm in perfect shape."

"I suppose it's just the light, then."

"Is there something wrong with the way I look?"

"You seem a little pale—that's all. My worst nightmare is having a scriptwriter keel over on me in the middle of a series, you know. At any rate, do take extra good care of yourself until we're through. Of course, after that, you can drop dead for all I care, but . . ."

We laughed, chatted awhile and then parted.

I looked at myself in shop windows as I walked along the street, but the reflection was never clear enough to show skin tone. I certainly didn't feel overworked.

Last night I had returned from dinner with my parents at a reasonable hour and was in bed by eleven. In the morning I'd sat down to read back through the manuscript at my usual nine o'clock starting time, and I'd finished in about an hour and a half.

The entire suggestion seemed ridiculous. And yet, it bothered me.

My mother and father belonged to the world of the dead, after all, and it did not seem implausible that a person who had contact with their kind would find himself sapped of his vital forces. Many such instances were found in the lore, from ancient legends to modern novels.

I hadn't noticed any change in my complexion when I shaved before going out, but it wouldn't be particularly surprising if I had indeed lost some of my color.

I was anxious to find a mirror to get a better look at myself. I wasn't afraid of what I might discover. Quite the contrary, I felt strangely at peace. Behind their easy-going nonchalance, my parents must have had to make sacrifices of untold proportions in order to come back and join me in this world. If it meant I needed to give up a portion of my lifeblood in exchange, I was quite willing to pay the price; in fact, it would actually be a load off my mind. Seeing for myself that I was paler than usual would let me breathe easier. My parents had been doing altogether too much of the giving.

I remembered an Indian restaurant I'd eaten at a number of times that had a large mirror on the wall next to the cash register. It was a bit early, but perhaps I would eat supper there before going on home.

If the new show was to start airing the second week of October, I wanted to write at least three more episodes before the end of August. That figured out to a pace of five days per episode. Whoa! Getting a little pumped up, are we? My lips bent in a crooked smile. No sign of flagging vitality there!

Nor did my face look the least bit sallow when I examined it in the mirror at the restaurant.

"You look dreadful," Kei said the moment she came in a little after nine that evening.

"What do you mean?" I responded, taken aback by her abruptness. I had checked myself in the mirror again after returning home and found nothing strange. "I wish you wouldn't tease me. Believe it or not, I'm actually kind of sensitive about my appearance."

I headed for the bathroom mirror, where I could examine myself in the brightness of two 100-watt, soft-white light bulbs.

"I admit that my age shows," I said, "but I don't think I look so dreadful."

Kei came up next to me and we stood gazing at our reflections side by side. Our eyes met in the mirror.

"The skin's sagging a bit under my eyes, but that's nothing new, and I think my color's about as good as you can expect for a forty-eight-year-old city slicker."

"Uh-uh," Kei said. "I watched you come in last night. When you got home."

"I thought I checked your window."

"And it was dark, right?"

"I figured you weren't home."

"I like to stand looking out my window, but I don't want people to see me like that and think I'm feeling down and out, so I usually turn out the lights."

"You should have called me."

"I was afraid."

"Of me?"

"You looked deathly pale."

"Now hold on just a minute. I want you to look at me right there in the mirror. You say I look bad. Sure, maybe I'd look pale if you put me next to some surfer boy. But this is pretty much how I've always looked, and I don't feel the least bit stressed out or tired. There's absolutely nothing for you to worry about. I'd appreciate it if you'd stop scaring me."

"If you can say that with a straight face," Kei said, "then there's really something wrong with you." Her eyes burned into me. "Are you telling me you don't see how haggard you are?"

"I look haggard? What're you talking about? In fact, I look much healthier than you!" I protested to the Kei in the mirror, my voice rising a pitch. "And I can see myself perfectly fine, thank you very much. Look. I'm raising my right arm, and now I'm lowering it. I'm putting it around your shoulder. I'm pinching my nose with my left hand and I'm sticking out my tongue. If I'm not seeing myself, then what the blazes am I seeing?"

"Stop being a wise ass!" The daggers in her gaze almost made me jump.

"I don't mean to be, but I'm also having a hard time taking this seriously. The fact is, I feel like I've got all the energy in the world right now. And every bit of that energy is standing here wanting you."

I pressed my lips to hers. Briefly she tried to pull away, as if wanting to say something, but then she yielded. After our lips parted, she spoke again.

"Has anything funny happened to you recently?"

"I'm not laughing, am I?" I asked, even though I knew exactly what she meant. If I told her about my parents now, she would jump to conclusions and denounce them as demonic spirits. I didn't want my parents to be spoken of as some evil to be exorcised.

"Tell me," Kei pressed me for an answer.

"No. I can't think of anything."

"You're lying."

"Why would you say that?"

"Because you're a lousy liar."

"When you glare at me like that, I feel like apologizing for lies I haven't told."

"Stop being evasive. I think something really serious is going on. I have a feeling about it."

"How exciting!"

"Stop kidding with me, will you?"

"I never realized you took my welfare so much to heart."

114

"Shouldn't that go without saying? Or have I been deluding myself?"

"About what?"

Kei hesitated a moment, ever so slightly averting her eyes. Then almost right away she returned her penetrating gaze.

"I've thought of us as being together, you know."

"I have too. It's just that . . ."

"It's just that what?"

"I'm in no position to assume we are."

"Why not?"

"There's a fifteen-year age gap between us."

"It's nice for a woman of thirty-three to be told she's too young, but I have a handicap, too, you know. So stop being so self-conscious. Are we lovers or not?"

"Of course we are."

"Then shall we continue our kissing somewhere other than in the bathroom?"

We enjoyed another long kiss there before moving back to the living room.

I thought we had put the issue of my health behind us.

But as we sat down on the sofa and I started to take her in my arms again, being careful not to touch her chest, Kei suddenly stiffened.

"You have to stop hiding whatever it is," she said.

"I'm not hiding anything."

"Then just answer me one thing."

"I promise you, you don't need to worry about me."

"You really, truly didn't look tired to yourself?"

"There's not a man on earth who doesn't show some wear and tear at age forty-eight."

"You have deep, dark bags under your eyes," she said, looking me in the face. "Your cheeks are hollow."

I gazed back at her silently.

"That's how you look right now. And it's how you looked in the mirror."

I'd once read a novel in which a perfectly healthy man becomes gravely ill when everyone he knows starts telling him how unwell he looks, but I couldn't imagine why Kei would attempt such a prank. Yet, the face I had seen in the mirror had had no deep, dark bags under the eyes nor any sunken cheeks. If anything, I would have said I looked a little overfed. That meant one of us had to be seeing wrong. If majority ruled, then it seemed Kei had the advantage, for my producer had also thought I looked gaunt.

I sat motionless as my mind raced. Kei, too, remained completely still, watching me.

A knot of terror throbbed to life in the pit of my stomach.

If the image I saw in the mirror was not my true reflection, then I had no way to diagnose my own condition. Could there be anything so preposterous? Yet, when I considered the other preposterous things that had been going on lately, I could hardly dismiss something just because it didn't accord with my own perceptions.

"All right, I'll tell you," I said. "I'll tell you all about it, but you have to promise not to think it's no good for me."

Kei silently nodded her head.

"It's been nothing but a blessing. I suppose I do look haggard and wasted, even if I can't see it myself. But I assure you there's no reason to worry in this case; it's unlike anything else that might affect my appearance. I've had a wonderful experience. Unreal, yes, I can't deny it, but also truly wonderful."

I began by telling her about the night I met my father at the Asakusa Variety Hall. She offered no sign of disbelief as she listened. I supposed she could be concealing her true reaction, lest I stop in the middle of my account, but even then it meant she was sincere about wanting to know.

Even if we were of the same mind about our relationship being more than casual, we hadn't actually been together so very long. It touched me deeply to see her listening with such earnestness, trying so hard to discover the cause of my emaciation. Though some would surely snicker, I must say I thought it was love.

As I spoke, I realized that I had not been cared for in a very long time. I wasn't being sore; I could hardly expect others to care about me when I had cared so little about others all these years. Only, I felt guilty that I was thinking of Kei's genuine concern as having broken a long dry spell.

For, only the day before, I had enjoyed the warm embrace of my parents' unconditional love.

Somewhere in my mind, I seemed to have accepted the experience with my parents as unreal while regarding my love for Kei as real, and I felt ashamed of myself.

This, in spite of reviewing everything my father had taught me about Flower Rummy after I got home last night—in spite of looking up "Flower Cards" in the encyclopedia and verifying that the cards were divided into months.

Yet, the longer I spoke with Kei, the more I felt that my mother and father's Asakusa could not possibly be real.

10

During the years of my marriage, everything I did had been influenced in one way or another by my wife. Even when she didn't try to tell me what I could or couldn't do, somewhere in the back of my mind I was forever considering how I would explain my actions to her. That constraint remained with me for a time even after my divorce, and I can still remember the amazing sense of emancipation I felt one day when all of a sudden I realized that what I chose to do was now nobody's business but my own.

The day after I told Kei about the events in Asakusa, I found myself once again in the clutches of that old constraint. I experienced anew the feeling of sneaking around behind someone's back.

I was contemplating a secret trip to Asakusa.

"Promise me," Kei had insisted the day before. "Promise me you won't ever go there again."

She pleaded with me endlessly, and I could find no sensible retort.

No matter how free of malice and mischief my parents' intentions might be, there could be no denying that they had long since passed into the world of the dead. The return of the dead fundamentally undermines the order of the living, and I wholeheartedly shared Kei's conviction that contact with such beings was something to be avoided. Yet, when it concerned my own mother and father, I could not bring myself to think of them as an evil to be fought.

"There's no way you can claim they're entirely benign, though," Kei rejoined. "I mean, your body is wasting away! You look absolutely shocking, with your eyes so hollow!"

Yet, when I returned to the mirror again that morning, I still could not see the emaciation she spoke of. "You have to believe me," she had said over and over. "You're nothing but skin and bones."

True enough, people sometimes failed to see their own decline even when it was plain as day to others. Perhaps there was a lesson for me in that truth, but I was in no mood to accept such an admonition from the mirror.

"Show me!" I cried to the mirror. "Show me how I really look!"

The mirror merely continued to reflect the same robust and ruddy countenance as before. And so long as that remained the case, I couldn't help wanting to go back and see my parents one last time.

"Come again!"

"Soon!"

"You can bet on it!"

That's what I had promised, and it seemed too cruel to simply stop showing up without any further notice. They could probably come to visit me here in my apartment if they had a mind to, but because of what I'd said as we parted last time, they would instead go on waiting expectantly at their home in Asakusa. To coldly abandon them in the name of self-preservation without so much as a word of farewell would be an act of gross selfishness. What was a little emaciation, anyway? Did my life really amount to so much that I could justify betraying my parents in order to protect it? Perhaps my relationship with Kei argued for the affirmative, but quite frankly, I no longer knew just how much stock I was willing to place in the love between a man and a woman.

My faith in parental love was similarly tenuous, and yet, in their current incarnation, my mother and father seemed to have come into this world solely for my sake. Not only that, I imagined their existence to be a most precarious one destined to vanish once and for all from this world the moment my heart ceased turning in their direction. I at least wanted to say good-bye.

And so with the approach of evening, I broke my promise to Kei.

By the time I finished outlining the plot for the second episode of the series, I had used up most of the afternoon. I called Kei's apartment to make sure she was not at home, then quickly made preparations to go out. In spite of this precaution, I had the uncomfortable feeling that she was watching my every move from somewhere nearby, and I attempted to shake off this sensation as I emerged into the hallway by saying out loud, "Let's see, now, where can I get something really good to eat?"

I had every reason to believe that Kei was in Tsukiji, sitting before a computer screen in the accounting department of the packinghouse where she worked. She couldn't very well take time off from work just to keep tabs on me. Since I'd even gone to the length of calling to make sure she wasn't home, I should have been able to watch the elevator doors open without experiencing that shrinking sensation in my stomach, and I should not have felt the need to conceal myself from Kei's window as I emerged from the entrance downstairs. Yet it was with exactly those feelings that I made my way outside and stole away from the building onto the busy thoroughfare.

I was surprised that it was taking me so much willpower to break my promise to Kei. Did it perhaps mean that I loved her more deeply than I had realized? In the cab on the way to Asakusa, I recalled the eyes that had drilled into me as she extracted my promise; I recalled, too, the lucent whiteness of her shapely buttocks.

"Hideo's here, dear."

As I came to the foot of the familiar metal staircase, I heard my mother's voice calling out overhead. Looking up, I saw her at the door of the apartment with a shopping basket looped over her arm. She nodded at me with a big smile and disappeared inside. Then I heard her call again.

"Hideo's come to visit, dear."

You'll annoy the neighbors shouting like that, I thought. But the truth was, I didn't know whether anyone besides me could even hear her voice.

By the time I reached the top of the stairs, my mother had re-emerged. She stood before the open door and welcomed me with a broad smile.

"Hello, dear."

"Hi, Mom." Her smile was contagious.

"I'm on my way to do some quick shopping," she said. "But Dad's inside."

I peered into the apartment after we slipped past each other and found my father pushing himself up to a sitting position. He had a paper fan in his hand.

"Yo," he said.

"Hi, Dad."

"Want some beer?"

He nimbly rose to his feet and went to open the refrigerator.

"Maybe we should save the beer for dinner."

"Aw, come on, don't be a spoilsport. I've been holding off all afternoon. I didn't want to hear Mom moan, so I've been drinking water and pretending it's beer, but all it does is make me feel bloated."

The high-school baseball tournament was on TV again. We sat cross-legged in front of the set and poured beer for each other.

"Played with anyone yet?"

"Played what?"

"Flower Rummy."

"I haven't had the time."

"You're too old to be saying you're too busy, you know. If you don't start enjoying yourself now, pretty soon it's gonna be too late."

"I was thinking maybe the three of us could try Nine's High today."

"I'll be your nanny. I guess I had it coming. I gotta take at least part of the blame when I find out my only son made it to a ripe middle age without ever learning his flowers."

My father then launched into a lesson on how to cheat. I was a captive audience as he demonstrated one method after another, and by the time my mother came back we had finished off three large bottles of beer between us.

Feeling a little tipsy, I turned a flushed smile toward my mother.

"Let's order in, Mom," I said.

"But I just went and bought all these groceries," she protested.

Yeah, sure you did. I'm quite aware it's all just a charade for my benefit.

"Take the night off, Mom," I said. "We'll order in, and you can play Nine's High with us."

"My word! If you aren't getting to be just like your dad!"

"What the hell's so bad about a son taking after his dad?" my father put in.

"Exactly," I said. "Let's order eel. It'll be my treat. I may not look it, but I'm doing pretty well. Better than the average guy, anyway."

"Well, perhaps I should go place an order, then."

"Not just around the corner," my father said. "Go to that place across from Katsumasa's."

"And I'm not talking about the plain eel rice bowls. Get some broiled livers, and their very best teriyaki eel, and some eel liver soup, with separate orders of rice." I tried to mimic the same finicky tone my father had used.

"What am I going to do with you two?" my mother said. "Ganging up on me like that." But I could tell she was pleased.

*

When she returned from placing the order, we all played Nine's High. My parents were both seasoned players and very quick with their cards.

"Make up your mind, make up your mind!"

"Come on, slowpoke."

"You gotta learn to slap 'em down with a little more flair!"

"Speak up! Do you want it or not? You're spoiling the whole rhythm of the game!"

Even though it was only a friendly game with their own son, they were fiercely competitive, and I was especially surprised by how the slang terms for the different scores rolled off my mother's tongue like second nature. Spitting the words out crisp and snappy, she was really quite the dame.

Later, as we savored our eel dinner, my father turned reflective. "You know," he said, "if we'd'a been around, we wouldn'a let you turn into such a know-nothing. But there's some things in this world you just can't do anything about."

"We couldn't very well teach flower cards to a boy of twelve, now, could we?"

"But be that as it may, it's always been my philosophy of life, or perhaps I should say my view of the human condition that—"

"My, my, aren't *you* full of fancy phrases all of a sudden," my mother interrupted.

"Aw, lay off, will you? I've read a serious book or two in my time, too, you know. It's just that I don't need books to tell right from wrong."

"Then why not just give it to us in your own words?"

"Can't you see I'm just trying to speak his language? I spend my days talking to all kinds on the other side of the counter, you know. If I didn't learn to speak their language, I'd never get anywhere. Sushi chefs don't have it half as easy as those French cuisine guys. We don't get to hide back in the kitchen feeling smug about the fancy food we're making and never giving the customer a second thought. We have to work right there in full view of the customer, day in and day out. It's like we're always on stage. We have to be actors, and we have to be chefs, and on top of that, we're on the front lines pushing our products, so we have to be salesmen, too. With all that to do, can you blame me for sometimes wanting to have a little fun? It's a high-stress job if there ever was one."

"I wonder," my mother said.

"Listen to her. That's the problem with women. They just stick their noses in the air and snort at all the trials and tribulations their husbands have to go through."

Not because they said anything in particular to show how much they cared about me, but rather because they seemed to be so heartily enjoying the time we spent together, and because they bantered back and forth so good-naturedly, in the end I could not bring myself to tell them that this would be my last visit. The subject remained unbroached when they saw me to the curb on International Avenue and sent me off with the same cheerful invitation as before.

"Come again!"

"We'll be expecting you!"

11

In the cab on my way home, I marveled at my parents' sense of moderation. They said whatever they wanted, but never so much as insinuated they'd love to come see me once. It saddened me a little, and even weighed on my conscience, that I had taken advantage of their reserve and not offered an invitation. But perhaps we were just subtly acknowledging that there was a line separating illusion from reality and that it must not be breached.

After a while I remembered my son Shigeki.

To say I "remembered" him no doubt makes me sound terribly aloof, but in fact, from around the time his mother and I started discussing divorce, my son had turned almost completely away from me. In a word, he had sided with his mother. He ignored me when I spoke to him, while continuing to speak with her as easily and familiarly as ever. I couldn't really fault him for this, since he knew he would have to live with her after the divorce; for that matter, if a boy of nineteen could develop a greater closeness to his mother as a result of his antipathy toward his father, perhaps it was best for me to abandon all efforts to win his affection. If it meant he would be a better son to his mother, then let him hate me. In essence, I decided then that I would try to forget my son.

By now, though, it seemed likely that Shigeki had learned of his mother's relationship with Mamiya. And if so, although perhaps college sophomores were old enough not to be prone to such emotional insecurities, I found myself wondering whether he might not be feeling the need for a father's love about now. After all, I'd taken to revelling in my own parents' love, and I could repay them by offering Shigeki the same.

"Sorry, but could you take me to Akasaka instead?" I said to the driver. I gave him the name of a hotel.

Staying in Akasaka would save me from having to lie to Kei at least for tonight. I would call Shigeki and ask him to come see me at the hotel tomorrow—perhaps for lunch. I would give him some extra spending money.

I didn't feel very sure, though, how Shigeki would receive such an unexpected overture from his father.

"Imamura residence," my ex-wife's voice said on the other end of the line. She'd gone back to using her maiden name.

"Hi, it's me."

She hesitated a moment. "Shigeki?"

"No, not Shigeki. Hideo."

"Goodness," she said, a strained smile coming into her voice. "It sounded a little bit strange for Shigeki, but I wasn't expecting to hear from you, so . . ."

"Right." It was my turn for a strained smile. This was the first time we'd spoken on the phone since the divorce.

"You two sound so much alike, it gives me the willies," she said.

"Sorry about that."

I had braced myself for some nasty exchanges, but somehow we weren't having a tense conversation.

"He's not at home?"

"He's in America. One of his friends is at a college in Arizona, on a one-year exchange program. Shigeki's spending three weeks of his summer vacation at the host family's."

"Arizona's awfully hot this time of year, isn't it?"

"He's young."

"You wanted him out of the way, didn't you?"

"What do you mean by that?"

"Does he know?"

"Does he know what?"

"About you and Mamiya."

"It's still too early to tell him."

"You're seeing Mamiya, right?"

"I'm under no obligation, you know."

"No obligation to what?"

"To tell you anything."

"Well, maybe not, but would it hurt to pay a little common courtesy? Mamiya and I were colleagues for a long time, but now we can't work with each other anymore."

"Go right ahead. Your private lives needn't interfere."

"It's not that simple."

"Oh, is that so? Well, you were the one who wanted the divorce, so whatever happens between me and Mr. Mamiya, you have no right to be jealous."

"I'm not jealous."

"Then you shouldn't be making such a big deal about it."

"Maybe not, but I bet Mamiya finds it awkward, too."

"He's said as much to me, but it's not as if he's committing adultery! I don't see why he has to feel so awkward about it when we've already divorced."

"But you were already seeing him before we split up, right?"

"How can you even imagine such a thing?"

"It all happened way too fast otherwise. You were in his arms barely a month after the divorce."

"You're disgusting. I'd been in the cold with you an awfully long time before the divorce came through. Someone could've whispered sweet nothings in my ear the very next day and I'd have fallen into his arms in an instant."

"Do you intend to marry him?"

"I told you, that's none of your business."

"Shigeki is my son, too. I have a right to be concerned about what effect it might have on him."

"Why should you be so concerned about that boy all of a sudden? You never paid him the least bit of attention before."

"I called because I wanted to see him."

"You really are disgusting. I'm sorry, but I have to hang up. Talking to you just makes me sick."

The line went dead with a *click*.

If you really find me so disgusting, then how about showing a little more gratitude at being rid of me? How about giving back a little of that dough you squeezed out of me?

Had she not already hung up the phone, I might well have gone on to make some such remark. She was right: I was disgusting. I couldn't help myself. My peevish side came shooting right to the surface like that every time I spoke with her. And she held up her end in kind. Somewhere along the line, that had become the inevitable pattern.

I had a single on the hotel's ninth floor. From my window I could see the lights in the windows of another high-rise hotel and the flow of cars snaking up and down Aoyama Boulevard.

It wasn't Shigeki's fault that I would be unable to see him. But as I gazed at the uninterrupted streams of white headlights and red taillights, I reflected on how familiar I had become with disappointment in my relationship with the boy.

From around the time he entered junior high, he seemed bent on disappointing me at every turn. This perception of mine probably owed as much to my own misguided expectations as to anything else, so in most cases I could not actually place the blame on him. Nevertheless, even though I knew that a young person's sense of self did not necessarily develop along the lines a parent might wish, it provoked my wrath when he ignored my feelings or talked back to me over some trivial issue.

But losing my temper with him proved fruitless, for it succeeded only in exhausting me, not in producing the desired change in his behavior. Around the time Shigeki entered high school I finally learned to accept the inevitable and shrug it off. After that, in undertaking any exchange with him, I always prepared myself for mild disappointment. It got to a point where if I asked him whether he'd like to have some coffee with me and he responded with a good-natured "Sure, Dad," as he did on occasion, I actually felt thwarted.

131

The fault lay with me, of course. For my failure both as a father and as a husband, the fault lay entirely with me.

Not that I truly believed that—but I found a small measure of satisfaction in painting myself black as I continued to gaze at the city lights from my hotel window.

The next morning I checked out a little after ten.

As I started across the lobby toward the entrance after paying my bill at the front desk, I caught sight of Mamiya coming into the hotel.

Knowing it would look odd if I suddenly veered off in a different direction, but at a loss for anything else to do, I simply halted and watched him stride in through the automatic doors. Perhaps he would not notice me, and if so, it would be just as well.

Once inside, Mamiya glanced about the lobby for a moment before turning toward the coffee shop. Then suddenly he stiffened and jerked his head back around to look directly at me.

Flashing a smile, I bobbed my head in greeting. It felt good to see him. Ayako's right, I thought. Surely there's no reason our private lives have to affect our working relationship.

"Hi," he said, barely opening his mouth and sounding very tentative. He stood motionless, still looking over his shoulder, staring at me with the eyes of someone who sees an apparition. Aren't you overdoing it a bit, I felt like saying as I walked toward him, but he quickly broke into a smile to dispel his surprise.

"Well, well," he said.

"What's up—so early in the morning?" I asked. Ten was an early hour for people who worked in television.

"I'm supposed to meet someone," he said glancing in the direction of the coffee shop. A man waved, and I recognized him as one of my fellow writers—a man several years my senior who was a much hotter property than myself at the moment.

Mamiya raised a hand in response, and I offered a small bow as well. After gesturing to us that we should take our time, the man settled back into his seat.

But I had nothing to say to Mamiya. Had it not been a freak encounter, I would no doubt have quickly found my tongue. I had to be circumspect about suggesting that we might try working together again.

"I could hardly believe my eyes when I recognized you a minute ago," he said.

"What do you mean? Even I have occasion to stay at a hotel now and then."

"No, I mean because of how much you've changed. And in such a short time."

"Changed?"

"It wasn't all that long ago that I visited you at your place. You look like you've lost an awful lot of weight since then."

"You think so?"

"Sorry if it's none of my business. It was just such a shock."

"I look like skin and bones?"

"Well, I don't know if I'd go that far, but what happened?"

"I suppose I might have pushed myself a little too hard."

"You need to be more careful."

"I guess now that I'm all alone, I don't know when to stop."

"Have you seen a doctor?"

"No. Since it's not as if I'm in any kind of pain." And since I don't appear the least bit changed to myself when I look in the mirror, I appended inwardly.

"I think you should."

"Don't you go trying to scare me now."

"No, really, I'm serious. You need to see a doctor. Forgive me, but losing so much weight so quickly definitely isn't normal."

"I suppose you're right. I will. So long," I said with a wave and started for the door.

"Where are you off to now?"

"Home."

Mamiya looked like he had something more to say, but I put him behind me and proceeded out the door.

The encounter confirmed what I had secretly suspected. The time spent with my parents last night had apparently made me even more emaciated in the eyes of those around me.

I walked toward the taxi stand.

Perhaps I was destined to go on wasting away, never able to see the ravages with my own eyes, until suddenly one day I dropped dead. So be it, then. One who's been given the chance to spend time with his departed parents must not ask for much more.

As usual, every last window in my building remained stoically closed against the engine roar and exhaust fumes rising from the vehicles plying Route 8.

Kei's window looked no different from any other. The glare of the late morning sunshine reflecting off it made it impossible to tell whether anyone was within.

Turning my key in the security panel, I pushed open the thick plate-glass door and went inside. A tall young man was standing guard next to seven or eight brand new cardboard boxes stacked neatly against one wall. I eyed him as I walked by, but he maintained his glassy-eyed stare and offered no response.

Stepping into the open elevator, I pressed the button for my floor. As the doors began to slide shut, I glanced toward the young man again and, to my surprise, found him staring at me with an odd look in his eyes. Though he averted his gaze as soon as our eyes met, I instantly recognized the look of curiosity. No doubt I had grown so withered in appearance as to attract most anyone's attention. Why could I still not see it? Was it some kind of trickery exercised by my parents?

The elevator stopped sooner than I expected—too soon for the seventh floor. I raised my eyes and saw the number three lit up over the door. Kei's floor. The doors opened. There she stood.

"Oh," I said in surprise. "Did you have the day off?"

She stood looking at me without a word. A sleeveless white dress flowed long like a negligée over her figure, reaching down to her ankles.

Since she didn't immediately step into the elevator, I pressed the "Open" button and smiled. "Well?"

A look of pity crept across a stricken face, as if what she saw truly broke her heart.

135

"Where have you been?" she asked, still not moving.

"I checked into a hotel to do some work. I needed a change of scenery."

"You're lying," she said, her voice low but firm. She kept her eyes locked on mine as she stepped into the elevator, approaching so close that I actually expected her to kiss me. "You're lying," she hissed again.

I caught the smell of sweet perfume. The doors closed behind her.

"This must be a first," I said gently as I returned her gaze. I pulled her to me but felt her stiffen under my touch. "The first time I've smelled perfume on you."

"I was watching from the window. I waited all night. You finally came home now." She said it very deliberately, almost as if she were reading the words out of a book. I sensed a note of anger.

"Are you playing hooky from work?"

Before she could answer, the doors slid open. She led the way down the seventh-floor hallway. I dug into my pocket for the key.

When Kei reached my door, she stepped to one side and stood tall and erect, watching my every move.

I unlocked the door.

"Let me go in first," I said. "I'll open the curtains and turn on the air conditioner. The heat just won't let up, will it?"

The way Kei had been glaring at me confirmed that my emaciation had indeed advanced, but I had no reason to behave feebly in accordance. I spoke with exaggerated cheer in my voice as I hurried to turn on the air conditioner and open the curtains. The steel door swung shut with a heavy, metallic sound.

"It's almost time for lunch, Kei. Shall we have some cold noodles? I bought a whole case of instant noodle packs the other day, and we also have the ham and cucumbers and eggs."

As I stood on a chair to adjust the slats on the air conditioner, Kei slid up to me and wrapped her arms around my waist.

"Why did you have to go? Why did you have to break your promise?" she said.

I considered my response, uncertain what to say, but I knew it would do me no good to lie.

"I wanted to tell them good-bye. I didn't want it to end, with me just suddenly not showing up anymore."

"And you did? You said your good-byes?"

I smiled awkwardly, still standing on the chair.

"Let go, will you? I want to get down."

But she would not let go.

"Answer me," she insisted. "Tell me you said your goodbyes."

"You're starting to sound like my mother."

"Stop being evasive. Did you tell them you couldn't come anymore?"

"I couldn't."

"I had a feeling."

"They haven't done a thing," I pleaded. "They haven't done anything to deserve that kind of news from their son."

Kei released her hold. "Get down," she ordered.

"I simply couldn't bring myself to say it." I stepped down from the chair.

"Come with me," she beckoned, her eyes burning into mine.

"Where?"

Impatiently, she clutched my right arm as if pulling on a rope and began dragging me toward the bathroom. She opened the door and flicked the switch. We stood side by side in front of the mirror as we had done once before.

"Can you see?"

"Of course I can see."

"And how do you look?"

The reflection in the mirror showed my usual, ruddy complexion.

"I look strong. My color is good."

"No!" Kei flung her arms tightly around my neck. "Somebody help this man! Please, oh please, oh please!"

Kei probably wasn't religious, but she was begging someone, and it wasn't me. She was imploring for some force to save me. The obvious sincerity of her appeal left me at an utter loss for words. I marveled at the discovery that there were people in this world who could pray so fervently for the welfare of another.

"Please," Kei continued to beseech at my ear. "Please, oh please, oh please help."

She was weeping. Kei was praying in tears.

I felt a surge of love and squeezed her tightly.

"Thank you," I said.

Kei merely continued her entreaties. "Please help," she said. "Please help this man. Please." She clung to my neck as if for dear life.

All at once a staggering sense of fatigue came over me. Kei weighed heavy on my shoulders. I could scarcely stay on my feet.

"Sorry," I said as my legs wavered under her weight. "I feel incredibly weak all of a sudden."

My legs gave way under me, and I could no longer hold her. I sank to the floor in a heap, gasping for breath.

"Are you all right?" She crouched down beside me.

"I don't know. For some reason, I feel utterly, utterly drained all of a sudden."

"You've got to look in the mirror."

What could she be talking about? Merely lifting my head required superhuman effort.

"Please! I think now you might be able to see. You have to look in the mirror."

See what? I can't even keep my eyes open. All I want is to lie down.

"You have to look in the mirror!"

She got to her feet and started pulling on my arm.

"I can't."

"Please! You have to!"

I managed to lift my head, and Kei struggled to raise me off the floor to the level of the mirror. Wedging a hand under my right arm, she wrapped herself around me and strained with all her might.

She finally lifted me just high enough, and I peered into

the mirror through the haze of my debilitating fatigue. I saw an old man. My heart skipped a beat. It was me.

The man with eyes sunk deep in their sockets, cheeks cavernously hollow, and skin as colorless as a pale white ghost, was me.

I screamed, "Ah!"

But the sound that emerged was only a feeble one, scarcely more than a sigh.

"Aaaa—"

I dragged myself on my hands and knees from the bathroom to the living room and rolled over onto the floor. The effort drained me of every last reserve of strength I had.

Kei came to lie beside me like a mother protecting her child. I closed my eyes and rested as tiny tremors shook my body. Terror gnawed at my stomach. Gone was my erstwhile bravado of being prepared to die for my parents. I chanted desperately in my heart: *Namu Amida Butsu, Namu Amida Butsu, Namu Amida Butsu*. O blessed Buddha! O blessed Buddha! O blessed Buddha!

12

My strength came back to me in about an hour.

I could feel the life flowing back into my limbs, surging like a rising tide to the tips of my fingers and toes. Soon I felt so full of vigor it hardly seemed possible I'd been too weak to stand only a short while before.

I opened my eyes and slowly turned my gaze to my hands. When I had apprehensively done the same a while ago, I had found ashen skin stretched grotesquely over little more than blood vessels and bones, but this time I discovered my normal fleshy hands. With that, a new burst of energy surged through me, and I could no longer hold still. I gently lifted myself to a sitting position.

"What is it?" Kei asked, her voice tender with concern.

"It's really weird," I said. "I suddenly feel normal again. Do I still look as bad as before?"

Kei nodded.

"I sure don't feel that way anymore. I feel like leaping to my feet and dancing around the room."

Her eyes filled with horror. And I immediately understood. The ghost of a man sitting before her now was in no condition to kick up his heels and dance except by some supernatural power that came from the world to which my mother and father belonged.

"Can I do anything for you?" Kei said, a mournful plea in her eyes.

"I'd like you to stay with me—if I don't give you the creeps."

"How can you say such a thing?"

"Sorry."

She was right, of course. After she'd clung to me and prayed for me, after she'd lain with me through my prostration, I'd treated her like a stranger. Yet, it seemed impossible that anyone could feel comfortable being with the wasted, pale-as-death specter of a man I'd seen reflected in the mirror—let alone hold him in her arms. Especially a man who was fifteen time-ravaged years older to begin with. Had I been in her place, I'd probably have let out a bloodcurdling screech and fled for dear life. Seeing how deeply she had come to care for me—not over years or even months but on the basis of a few nights—was a sharp rebuke to me. I had been wrong about people. About women too.

"Thank you," I said. But I could not bring myself to look at her. I would have liked to give her my most grateful smile and throw my arms around her, but I knew that bending my ghostly lips would serve only to magnify the ghoulishness of my appearance.

"I'm getting hungry," I said.

"I'll make something." She rose to her feet and went into the kitchen.

I now felt so full of energy again that I wanted to pitch in, but I decided it was probably better if she had some time to herself.

By the time we finished lunch and lingered briefly over a cup of coffee it was after two. We had spent the entire time talking about other matters.

Kei had always imagined that television writers had a wild social life. I told her that some did, but that for the most part the task of writing demanded long stretches of solitude. I described for her a short story by Paul Theroux about the social lives of writers in London that quite comically reveals how very alone and isolated each of them is in spite of all their carousing. For my part, I wasn't at all inclined to ridicule a writer's isolation. Nor did I suffer from being alone.

"Really?" Kei asked.

"I still want you with me," I hastily added. "Your being here has been a terrific help."

But inwardly, I had to admit that her question had touched a nerve. Perhaps I wasn't as comfortable with my solitude as I liked to think. Perhaps I had wanted to be on my own again purely to escape the shackles of wife and child, and now that I'd actually regained my independence, I was discovering that I wasn't really so independent after all. I had not consciously felt lonely, but it may well have been my own subconscious loneliness that had summoned my mother and father back into this life from the world of the dead.

Our coffee cups were empty when the conversation finally turned back to them.

Kei fell silent.

And so did I. The entire time we'd been talking of other things, I'd been wondering what to do.

Suddenly from the street came the long, loud screech of a panic-stricken driver slamming on his brakes. Anticipating the crash, I instinctively turned toward the window. Kei did the same.

But no crash came—only the usual din of traffic, thundering on and on.

"Tonight," I said.

"Yes?"

"I need to go to Asakusa one more time."

"It could kill you."

"I'll die anyway at this rate."

"Do you really think so?"

"You say these hands of mine are like skin and bones, but that's not what my eyes tell me. I can't just decide not to see my parents again and expect that to be the end of it."

"But maybe you should give it some time. Maybe their power over you will diminish, and then maybe it can be the end of it."

"That feels wrong, somehow. It might leave them in limbo, keep them from crossing peacefully back to the other side. That's what I'm worried about. I don't want it to end with me simply abandoning them. They're good folks."

"They've been sucking the lifeblood out of you."

"I don't think they ever meant to. I think that's just what intercourse between our different worlds does to you. My parents probably don't have any idea I'm dying. They probably can't see me wasting away any more than I can. In fact, I'm sure of it. Otherwise, they'd have said something by now."

"You're so understanding."

She did not intend it in a good way. Quite uncharacteristic-ally, she was being sarcastic.

I said: "I hope you won't think I'm a hopeless case, but . . ."

"What?"

"I have to go to Asakusa one last time—precisely because I think you and I have got something going and I value it."

"And how does your dying help us?"

"I can't very well go to the police for something like this."

"But how about a priest, maybe a shaman?"

"This is my parents we're talking about. I'm not going to pay an exorcist to get rid of them."

"You're being too idealistic. Real families aren't that pretty, you know."

"I lost my parents when I was twelve. Excuse me if my view is rosy."

"Give me a day. I'll get some advice."

"Where?"

"I haven't decided. The church. Wherever."

"I'm sure of it."

"Sure of what?"

"That they'll understand."

"No, that's what you *hope*. Are you really willing to stake your life on nothing more?"

"Don't worry. I'll be fine. I'll be back by ten or eleven."

Kei stood up.

"At least give me until four o'clock."

"No."

"Three-thirty then." It touched me how desperately she

wanted to help. "Don't go anywhere until three-thirty, okay? Promise me that." She ran for the door. "Promise me you won't go anywhere."

The heavy door swung open and then shut again.

To Kei, my parents were vengeful spirits to be shunned at all costs. Knowing that she regarded them that way saddened me, and I felt sorry for my parents. Who'd side with them if I didn't?

I strode to the window. Kei would be emerging soon. At this moment, the elevator was probably still on its way up. Or perhaps it had just now reached my floor and slid open. Yes, now she would be stepping into it. The doors close. The elevator begins its descent.

Suddenly Kei rushed out from the building—much sooner than I expected. Wearing only her long, white housedress and a pair of slip-on sandals, she ran onto the street. The slightness of her shoulders remained with me after she disappeared from view.

I may never see her again, I thought, then slowly turned toward the door.

13

"Hey there! You're here two days in a row!"

My father greeted me with a bright smile from the kitchen sink, where he had pulled his arms from his yukata robe sleeves to wipe himself down with a cool washcloth.

"I hope you're not taking after your father and neglecting your work," my mother chided as she busily reorganized the futon closet.

"I brought half a watermelon," I said, setting the plastic grocery bag on the kitchen floor. "I thought a whole one would probably be too much."

"Better get it in the fridge," my father said.

"It's already chilled," I said as I stepped out of my shoes. "They had them on ice."

"In that case, maybe we should eat it right away." My mother got to her feet and came into the kitchen.

"In that case we should most definitely eat it right away," my father said, pushing his arms back through his yukata as he slipped past my mother into the other room. "Ahh, watermelon—good call!"

"Quite a heat wave we're having," my mother said as she turned the faucet to wash her hands. "I think I'm getting a rash around my neck."

"Yo, don't just stand there, Hideo. Take your shirt off. Make yourself comfortable," my father called.

"I thought maybe we could eat out tonight. What do you think?" I said as I went to join him.

"Out?" my mother turned to look at me.

"I don't think we ever had sukiyaki at a restaurant," I said.

"No way we could afford anything like that back then," my father said. He was adjusting the position of the fan after setting it to oscillate.

"That's why I was hoping you'd let me take you out tonight," I said.

"Instead of eating here?" I discerned a note of tension in my mother's voice. My father had stopped what he was doing.

"Would you rather we just ate here?" I asked, already preparing to withdraw the proposal, but my father seemed to be warming to the idea.

"Not really," he said.

"But, dear," my mother objected, standing stiff and motionless in the kitchen.

My father and I had gone up the street a ways to play catch the other day, and I'd assumed that going a little farther afield to a sukiyaki place down by Kaminarimon Gate wouldn't be a problem either. But they were reacting as if I'd asked them to cross a daunting barrier.

"Let's forget it then. It was just a thought."

I didn't really want to say good-bye at the apartment. I figured it would be easier to broach the subject somewhere like the main dining room of a sukiyaki restaurant, for example, where we would be surrounded by crowds of other customers and wait staff. But I'd trash the plan if it was inconvenient for my parents.

"It's not exactly the season for sukiyaki anyway," my father said. "We can eat something here."

"Yes, let's do that," I agreed. "I just thought it might be fun to have a festive hot-pot feast together—that's all."

"I don't know about doing a hot-pot here, without air conditioning," my mother said.

"No, you're right. Really. Let's forget it. I'm sorry I even brought it up."

"Don't just stand there. Hurry up and cut the watermelon," my father scolded Mom. My suggestion had thrown cold water on what had started out as a perfectly cheerful occasion. I realized how fragile our tranquil little world actually was.

Today, however, I could not let that sway me. I had to break the news to them, no matter how severe the blow.

"I felt like coming back so soon."

"Sure, why not?" my father said. "Come as often as you like."

"Of course," my mother concurred.

"How about a round of cards?" my father asked.

"All right," I replied. "But let's have our watermelon first."

Part of me feared that my mother and father might turn into grotesque monsters and begin assailing me viciously the moment I declared I could not come again. I shrank from that prospect, and yet I also believed that if such a thing did occur, they would regard it with the same horror as I did; it would not be anything they had willed to happen.

We finished our watermelon and got out the cards.

My mother quickly shed the shadow that had come over her earlier and played her usual mean hand.

Four o'clock came, then five o'clock.

I kept thinking I needed to call a halt, but they both seemed to be enjoying the game so much I couldn't bear to. Evening twilight began to creep into the room.

Suddenly, I broke out in a cold sweat. I had to speak up while it was still light. My courage might fail me once darkness fell, and I simply could not leave Asakusa today without saying my last good-byes.

"I guess we could use some light," my father said, standing up to reach for the pull switch. "What time is it, anyway?"

"It's a little after six," my mother replied.

Light filled the room, and the twilight glow disappeared from the window.

"I'd better go do some shopping for dinner," my mother said.

"It's kinda late to be thinking of that now, don't you think? Just throw something together from yesterday's leftovers."

"That's all gone. We had it for lunch, remember? Except for some fermented soybeans."

"Don't be ridiculous. We can't serve Hideo a dinner like that."

"Dad," I said. "Mom."

"Yeah?"

"Don't worry, dear. I'll have dinner for you in a jiffy. I'll figure something out while you and your dad have some beer."

"There's something I have to tell you."

"Something to tell us?"

"What is it?"

"I'm sorry. Is it okay? Is now a good time?"

"Can't say it's particularly good, but shoot."

I uncrossed my legs and shifted to a formal kneeling position, then lowered my head in a deep bow.

"Is something wrong?" My mother seemed concerned.

"What's this about?" my father said, as he, too, dropped to his knees.

"I won't be able to visit you anymore after today."

"Why not, dear?"

"Whadda ya mean?"

Their voices rose in unbelieving protest, as though I'd said something sadly absurd. As I had suspected, they knew nothing of my enfeeblement.

"I've really loved coming here, and you can't imagine how happy it's made me to see you again. So in some ways I'd like to keep coming even if it does kill me."

"Kill you? What're you talking about?"

"Yes, dear. What makes you say a thing like that?"

I recounted for them what my producer and Mamiya had said about my health, and described the wasted figure I had seen in the mirror.

I left Kei out. This required a certain amount of fabrication, but it seemed the safer course to follow. Even if my parents showed no ill will toward her, someone perceived as trying to separate me from them could potentially suffer retribution from unknown powers in the world of the dead. Of course, I

151

was far from certain that saying nothing about Kei would protect her, but my mother and father did appear to be buying my story.

As I finished my narrative, I once again bowed deeply in apology, my palms on the floor.

Neither of them said a word.

Cards remained scattered on the cushion we had been using as our playing surface.

I could not lift my head. I had a chilling feeling that my mother and father had already taken on a terrifying new aspect and were poised to pounce on me. My entire body shook.

But my fears were unwarranted.

"I see," my father said gently.

"I have to admit," my mother sighed, her voice filled with sadness, "I had a feeling this couldn't go on forever."

I still could not bring myself to lift my head. I wanted to simply evaporate into nothingness.

"What can't be helped can't be helped," my father sighed.

"That's right," my mother said. "But brief as it was, we can't tell you how happy we were to have you with us."

"Whadda ya say we go after all?" my father suddenly perked up.

"Excuse me?" I lifted my head in surprise at the change in his tone.

"You know, for sukiyaki. Who cares if it's the middle of the summer? If we go to a restaurant, we can stuff ourselves with sukiyaki in air-conditioned comfort."

"Are you sure it's okay?" I asked.

"Of course it's okay," my mother said, choking back a sob. "We're saying good-bye, aren't we? Of course it's okay."

In the deepening dusk, the three of us made our way along the sidewalk toward Kaminarimon Gate. After crossing International Avenue we passed a lamprey eel shop where an attendant was grilling skewered livers out front.

"Let's each have one of those," my father said, halting his steps.

Hearing him speak made me realize none of us had uttered a word since leaving the apartment.

"Sounds good to me," I said, putting a little extra bounce in my voice.

"Three please," my father said to the attendant.

"But we're on our way for sukiyaki," my mother protested. She still sounded a little choked up.

"Don't be a spoilsport. This boy needs all the nourishment he can get. You know that."

"You're gonna love it, Mom," I said, handing her a skewer.

"Thank you, dear."

We all fell silent again as we continued along the sidewalk eating.

As if to disperse the gloom, my father suddenly said "Say!" and halted his steps again.

"What?" I said, putting on the most cheerful face I could muster.

"They were selling figurine cakes back there. How about we get ourselves a bag?"

"Sure. You guys keep walking. I'll catch up in a minute."

I retraced my steps to buy a bag of the small cakes shaped like the Sensoji temple and the seven deities of good fortune and such. As I waited for my change, I turned to see how far my parents had gone and found them waiting for me exactly where I'd left them. Making a purchase while my thirty-something parents watched made me feel like I was a kid in junior high.

That's right, I realized. For my parents, to part with me was also to part with Asakusa. Today they were bidding adieu to their beloved hometown too. My father wanted the cakes because he was trying to make the most of his last trip down memory lane.

I hurried to rejoin my parents. "Dad," I said as I trotted up, "the hard-baked rice crackers at the place on Sushi Shop Alley!"

"Sounds great!"

"It'll only take a minute, Mom," I said, and dashed off.

I found the shop up a short alley in the direction of the movie district, but the crackers I wanted were sold out for the day. A fine time for them to be sold out!

When I ran back, my parents looked rather forlorn standing amidst the flow of pedestrians on the sidewalk.

"They were all sold out," I said. "It sucks." I was pushing fifty, but I griped like a kid in junior high.

"Oh, well," my father shrugged it off, trying to sound cheerful to cover up his disappointment.

My mother simply stood gazing at me.

"Shall we go on up to the temple and offer a prayer to the Goddess of Mercy before we have dinner?" I asked. "We can munch on our little cakes while we browse the shops along the way."

"I really wish we could," my father said, obviously unhappy that he had to turn the suggestion down. "I really wish we could, but we're not at liberty to do just anything we please."

"Yes, wouldn't it be nice if we could?" my mother said, tears spilling from her eyes. Her shoulders sagged so, it was hard to believe she was the same person who'd played cards with such animation only an hour ago. I literally had to swallow the words that tried to leap off my tongue: Forget it, forget it. Forget what I said about this being my last visit. I'll come again, Mom. I will.

That was what I longed to say but didn't.

When my father asked if we should be going, I answered, "Yes! Let's go and have ourselves some sukiyaki. Let's make it a real feast."

"Come right in!" the seventyish shoe-check woman welcomed us in a deep, resonant voice as we entered.

"We'd like a table for three," I said.

"Yes sir," she said, then called out, "Seating for a party of three, please."

"Coming," we heard from inside, and moments later a plump, fair-skinned waitress who looked to be in her forties came shuffling out to greet us.

"Welcome," she said, "Right this way, please."

Rows of low tables outfitted with built-in gas burners filled a large hall. Decorative screens about a meter tall

155

surrounded each table on three sides, providing privacy for the diners.

There were plenty of open tables. At a quick glance, I guessed fewer than half the cubicles had steam rising from them.

This is just about perfect, I thought. A house so full that the drunken revelers next door might come crashing through the screens was fine in the winter, but a crowded hall in the summer would seem too close even with air conditioning.

The waitress led us to a table against the back wall, and I sat down facing my parents. We ordered some beer along with the most expensive sukiyaki dinner for three.

"And we'll be ordering lots more meat and vegetables as we go," I added.

"Just let me know when," the waitress said. "I'll be right back with the beer." As she rose from her knees, I noticed perspiration dotting her forehead.

"You didn't really need to say that," my mother said dispiritedly.

"Don't make a fuss," my father said to her, annoyed. "Just don't make a fuss."

"But what'll we do with so much food?"

"Nobody said you had to eat it. Don't forget, this boy's been wasting away a little more with every visit. We may not be able to see it, but he's really worn out."

"I know that."

"Then stop giving him a hard time when he's only trying to build up his strength."

"Never mind me," I said. "I want you guys to eat to your heart's content."

"Stop talking like you're in an honor-your-parents civics class," my father snapped. "Look, I can't say this very loud, but eating piles of thin-sliced beef ain't gonna put meat on a dead man's bones. The figurine cakes were plenty for me."

"But you can still savor it for its taste, right?"

"Sure, I'll love every bite."

"Then I say let's all eat up."

"Well hey, I suppose we may as well. It's only while we're with you that we can eat."

The beer arrived.

"Say, sis," my father said to the waitress. "What would you say we look like here?"

"Husband and wife, I imagine."

"Oh, right, that goes without saying. But I didn't mean us, I meant him. What's his connection?"

"One of your regulars, maybe?"

"Whadda ya mean, regulars?"

"Well, like, maybe you're a chef or something in a restaurant."

"Whoa! You've got quite an eye."

"And he's one of your regular customers, invited you out to dinner today."

"Bingo!"

The waitress laughed and went away.

"This isn't the time to be playing games with a waitress," my mother said, looking quite miserable.

"Look who's talking. Here I am, doing my level best to

157

liven up the party, and you just keep throwing cold water on everything."

"How can you sit there acting so gay?"

"Let's let it rest, Mom," I said. "There's no reason you should have to force yourself to be cheerful, but I can understand how Dad feels, too, so how about we put away the barbs and drink up."

Lifting a bottle from the table, I filled their glasses with beer.

"No one would ever guess you were our son," my father said with a forlorn smile as he poured for me. "Strange things do happen."

I didn't think "Cheers!" would quite fit the occasion, and any other toast I offered would probably put my mother in tears, so I just raised my glass and said, "Well, then," and we all took our first draft.

The waitress returned. She placed a sukiyaki pan on the burner in the middle of the table and greased it, then began preparing the sukiyaki.

"Let me tell you a little something about this kid," my father said to the waitress.

"My goodness! Are you sure you wanna call him that?"

"Oops, you're right."

"It's okay, it's okay," I said. "I like it when he does that."

"He lost his parents when he was twelve, you see."

"I'm so sorry!"

"And after that he went through some pretty tough times. But he made good. He really made good. He's got a lot to be proud of."

"So you had to fend for yourself from when you were little?" the waitress looked my way.

"Not at all," I said. "First my grandfather took me in, and after he was gone my aunt and uncle looked after me."

"But still, he was basically on his own most of the time," my father insisted. "He had to make everything happen for himself. And look at him. He's a big success. He can come to a place like this and order up all the beef he wants."

"Goodness sakes, you're not drunk already, are you?" the waitress exclaimed, surprised by my father's fervor.

"Thank you, that'll be fine," my mother said. The sudden cheer in her voice nearly made me jump. When I turned to look at her, she went on speaking to the waitress with a bright smile. "I can handle the rest. We'll let you know if we need more of anything."

"Oh, thank you," the waitress said without missing a beat. "We're actually a little shorthanded right now because two of our young people went back home for the Bon festival and never came back." She bowed politely and withdrew.

My father pointed after her with his chin. "Be sure to drop a bill on her on the way out," he said.

"All right," I said.

"They don't do that anymore, dear. That's American."

"Sure they do. Some people still like to show their appreciation, you know. One small bill is all it takes. A hundred yen. No, no, they don't even make hundred yen bills anymore. The small bill these days is a thousand. I can't believe it! A thousand yen for a tip. Man! Such fine times you live in, Hideo! What's the world coming to?"

159

"Maybe I don't need to say this after all this time, but—" my mother spoke up again, gazing straight at me.

"Don't bet on it," my father interjected as he poked at the simmering food in the pan with his chopsticks. "If you've got anything you want to tell him, now's the time to do it."

"I still can't believe you're forty-eight years old!"

"I know what you mean," I nodded. "For my part, I was thrilled to see you so young and pretty."

"Says a son to his own mother?" My father looked a little embarrassed. Perhaps I would not have paid my mother such a commonplace compliment had I been my father's age. But at the moment I felt as though the commonplace was exactly what the situation demanded. It seemed the best way to convey my feelings.

"I can't get over how you managed all by yourself for thirty-six years," my mother said.

"Don't forget, he did have a wife for a good while," my father pointed out.

"I guess children find a way to muddle through one way or another even when their parents aren't there."

"If their parents aren't there, they haven't really got a choice, do they?"

"Will you shut up just for a minute, dear?"

"What're you talking to me like that for?"

"Don't you realize? There's too little time left for you to be wisecracking." My mother's voice suddenly began to tremble. She seemed on the verge of tears.

"What do you mean, too little time?" I said, looking from my mother to my father. "Are you in some kind of a hurry?"

"Yes, we need to hurry," my mother said, tears now spilling from her eyes. "That's why I sent the waitress away."

I turned back to my father, who looked as though he'd taken a slap in the face.

"What's this about?" I asked.

"It's nothing," he said, shaking his head in vehement denial. But the look on his face told me otherwise.

"Now listen," my mother said, shifting in her seat to a more formal position. "I'm feeling pressed and can't say it very well, but we both care about you so much."

"You're not leaving already, are you?"

I had a feeling that they were.

"It was really good meeting you again," my father said. "You're a fine son."

"Yes, you are a fine son."

"No I'm not," I protested. "I'm nothing like the man you two seem to think I am. I failed as a husband, and I wasn't much of a father, either. You two are fine folk—not me. You're warm, so warm I was surprised. Everyone should have parents like you, my son included. And though I've played the devoted son with you, there's no telling how I might have treated you if you'd lived all these years. My career? I've never produced anything truly great. I'm just a hack competing for—"

I broke off mid-sentence.

Something was happening to my mother. I could see the shape of her shoulders clearly enough, but I realized I could also see right through them.

Stunned, I turned to look at my father. His shoulders and torso were beginning to fade as well.

This was what my mother meant. This was how they were going to leave me. The shock was so great that I just sat there, unable to speak.

"It's all right, son," my father said. "Don't say another word."

"We're so proud of you," my mother said.

"So proud," my father echoed. "Do us a favor and stop being so hard on yourself. A man's gotta stand up for himself, you know. No one else is gonna do it."

"Please don't go," I pleaded, my voice suddenly like a small child's.

"Looks like that's not for us to decide," my father said. "I was hoping we'd have at least a little more time . . ."

"No!"

"Take good care of yourself."

"I don't suppose we'll ever see you again."

My father's shoulders had disappeared, and my mother's face was growing dim. I knew I could do nothing to stop it. I dared not look away. My father was about to go.

"Thank you," I said. "Thank you! Thank you Mom and Dad!" My voice was hushed. The last thing I needed now was the attention of the waitress or the other guests.

"Good-bye," my mother said. I could hardly see her.

"So long," my father said. I couldn't see him at all.

I was too devastated even to cry.

"Good-bye," I murmured.

So quickly, my mother and father vanished without a trace, leaving behind only their chopsticks and sukiyaki bowls and half-empty glasses of beer, a bag of figurine cakes, a soiled table, and two wrinkled cushions.

A cloud of steam rose over the simmering sukiyaki in the pan.

"But you hardly ate," I moaned in protest. "Hardly a bite." Suddenly I felt exhausted.

I ached to let my head sink to the table, but I propped my elbows in front of me and cupped my face in my hands.

"Oh," I heard the waitress say. "I hope they found the restrooms all right."

"They left."

I lowered my hands but kept my face averted. I had to assume I looked even worse now than before, and I didn't want to frighten her.

"They both left?"

She obviously thought something had gone wrong. What else could she think? The meal remained virtually untouched.

"Please bring me the check," I said.

"You're not going to eat?"

"No."

"I must apologize. I'm afraid I didn't even notice them getting up to go," she said. "Well, I'll be right back with your bill, then. Shall I turn the burner off?"

"Yes, please."

"What in the world happened? They seemed to be enjoying themselves."

I could not hide my distress from her. The waitress turned off the gas and left to tally up our bill.

I had no time to be crying. I wanted something to remember them by. Their chopsticks. Desperately clawing my way through the leaden shroud of fatigue, I gathered up the two pairs of chopsticks they had used. Then I drew a handkerchief from my pocket and concentrated all my strength on carefully wrapping them up.

"I'm sorry to keep you waiting," the waitress said, returning with the bill.

It took an enormous effort to find the total, take out my wallet, and count out the correct number of bills.

"Are you feeling unwell?" the waitress asked, her voice quivering. She had obviously noticed my wasted countenance.

"Here." I handed her the money, and she promptly headed back to the cashier's station.

Slowly, I rose to my feet. After taking four or five steps down the aisle toward the main hallway, I turned for one last look. Our table sat there like an empty cicada shell, desolate.

I thought maybe I should take the figurine cakes, too, but I didn't have the strength to return for them.

When I reached the hallway, I waited for the waitress to come back with my change. As my father had instructed, I gave her a ¥1,000 note and some small change as a tip.

"Customer departing. Number twenty-three," she called out to the shoe-check lady as I proceeded toward the entrance foyer.

I wondered if my parents' shoes would still be with mine, but they had disappeared. The elderly shoe-check lady retrieved my lone pair of shoes and set them out for me with no sign that anything was amiss.

"Please come again!" she said in the deep voice I remembered from when we arrived. She had no way of knowing what I'd just been through.

14

Out of the darkness came the delicate scent of a woman's perfume.

In its depths the scent concealed a faint smell of flesh, which I was invited to discern, as it were, under the camouflage. Camouflage is designed to hide, but that seemed a mere pretense now as it seduced me to seek what it hid. As I slowly returned to consciousness, the scent of the perfume gradually grew fainter, and I became aware of the sweet smell and warmth of a woman's body enfolding me.

I opened my eyes in slits and saw white flesh. The knowledge that I was wrapped in it was very pleasant.

"How do you feel?" I heard Kei say.

Ahh, it's Kei. "Mmm," I grunted.

"Are you feeling any better?"

I wondered what time it was. I felt like I'd been sleeping for eons.

When I arrived back from Asakusa by cab, Kei had rushed to my side in the lobby to offer a supporting shoulder. But I had rudely pushed her away. I tried to walk alone.

Though I knew she deserved an explanation, I lacked the strength to speak. I had just then returned from saying goodbye to my parents, and it seemed wrong to fall straight into the arms of a waiting woman. I wanted to distance myself from any connotations of sex.

Kei could not read my mind, of course, and her eyes betrayed how hurt she was by my rebuff. But she hovered close by as if to form a protective circle around me as I walked, and she got into the elevator with me. Though it is odd to speak of a single person forming a circle around me, that was precisely how it felt; she seemed braced to catch me no matter which way I fell. I knew I owed her my gratitude, but perversely I felt much the opposite.

I brushed her helping hands aside again when my legs started to buckle as I stepped from the elevator into the seventh-floor hallway. I shouldn't have done it. Why be cruel to her? She'd done nothing wrong. But I refused her help yet once more when I sank weakly to my knees at my front door after failing to get the key I'd dug out of my pocket into the keyhole.

Now I lay in my bed.

I could not remember how I had gotten there. Nor could I say whether I'd finally been able to open my own front door. I recalled only my stubborn rejection of Kei's attempts to help me. But now that feeling was only a memory as I lay in Kei's embrace. I didn't seem to mind at all.

"How do you feel?" Kei asked again.

"Mmm."

"Do you still feel weak?"

Well, let me see. I don't think so. No, I definitely don't feel so tired and feeble anymore. I opened my mouth to tell her this, but instead my lips pressed against the white flesh before my eyes as though drawn there by an irresistible force. It was the small expanse of flesh just below Kei's collar bone and

166

above the broad, white elastic-bandage that continued to conceal what lay beneath. I quickly came to the bandage as I moved my lips across her tender skin, and I reached to pull the annoying impediment aside.

"No," Kei said sharply.

"I told you before," I said. "No scars could ever change how I feel about you."

"I'm sorry, but you mustn't. Never."

She trembled as she crossed her arms over her chest and rolled onto her stomach, her delicate white shoulders stiff with tension.

It's okay. Why can't you have more faith in me? I put my hand on her shoulder. "It's okay. Relax. You needn't worry," I said. I gently caressed the whiteness of her shoulder, then brought my lips to it. I touched it with my tongue. The smooth white slope of her back was covered with the same fabric that hid her chest, but I did not try to pull it away again.

My hand slowly descended the slope of her back and peeled away the tangled folds of blanket that concealed her bottom. Her naked white buttocks rose in two tense mounds, twisted slightly to one side. Delighting in their beauty, I touched them, caressed them, kissed them, drowned in them.

In the midst of our ensuing abandon, Kei gasped out, "It's over?"

"Yes, it's over. They're gone."

In the broken breaths with which I assured her that my mother and father were gone, there was only the faintest trace of parting's sorrow.

We went out for lunch a little after three.

The mid-afternoon heat was intense. Because the air stood so thick with car and truck exhaust, it had become my habit to curb my breathing. But I was enjoying the outing.

Kei apparently did not share my enjoyment. As we hiked toward the small Spanish restaurant a full kilometer down Route 8, she voiced a thinly veiled complaint.

"Why don't you have a car?"

"I did, but I gave it to my son," I said. "Once I finish the new series I just started, I should be able to afford something along the lines of an Accord again."

"Promise?" Kei pleaded.

"Sure thing," I said. "And we can look for a new apartment, too."

"Some place without all this constant noise."

"And with more room."

"But our new building still gets to be just the two of us at night."

When we reached the restaurant, we learned that they served only coffee until five-thirty.

"We do also have some pastries," the proprietress added with a smile.

By this time neither of us had the energy to leave the air-conditioned restaurant and wander along the scorching sidewalk in search of a square meal. We decided to settle for coffee and tarts.

The restaurant was empty except for one other couple, and we chose a table that was far away from theirs. As we settled into our seats, the view of sun-beaten Route 8 outside the window seemed like a scene from a different world. It was quiet inside; even the usual background music had been turned off. A cat ambled slowly across the hushed mid-afternoon eatery.

My mother and father would never get to see this view, I thought, as grief finally began to assert itself.

"It isn't going to be enough for you, I can tell," Kei giggled.

"What's not enough?"

"The little tart. You know, after not eating anything since last night."

"It never entered my mind," I said without smiling. I was annoyed by Kei's oblivious good cheer. When my parents had sacrificed their very being for me!

But in truth I had not yet filled her in on the events of the night before. I felt I needed more time before I could relive those events in all their heart-wrenching detail. So I could hardly blame Kei for rejoicing as though some dangerous, vengeful spirits had been summarily exorcised. It wasn't really that Kei was annoying me. I was feeling guilty about my eagerness to begin a whole new happy life with her. I banished my parents and was sitting here the next day enjoying the company of a ravishingly beautiful woman.

"There's something I need to tell you," I said.

"Uh-oh," Kei said with a smile. "I think I'm scared."

"I've already failed as a husband once. And I guess I wasn't a very good father, either. I'm not sure I deserve to be loved by someone like you."

"So?"

"I'd rather you didn't have any illusions about me."

"Like what?"

"I don't know, but I sometimes wonder what it is that you see in me. I worry that you haven't seen the real me."

"Everybody has illusions."

"Of course. And I'm not much of a man, I'm telling you."

"And I guess you want me to tell you that that's perfectly fine?"

"I suppose."

"Well, no, sir. If you're not much of a man, then make yourself more of one. I'm not going to rubber-stamp you as you are. You won't get off that easy, ha!"

She was right, of course. My parents had affirmed me as I was no matter how much I rejected myself, even as they faded into nothingness; but it was unwise to expect the same of a lover.

"I don't want this to sound . . ." Kei began with a faint smile, but stopped short when our coffee and tarts arrived. I reveled in her beauty as she waited with slightly downcast eyes for the proprietress to leave.

"You were saying?" I urged her to go on.

Kei nodded and started over. "I don't want this to sound like I think I'm special or anything, but—"

"You certainly are," I jumped in. "You're bright, and you're beautiful, and you're engaging, and you have a strong sense of who you are."

"But I've probably been showing you only my very best side. Hiding my chest is pretty plain proof of that."

"I'm not into self-deprecation, but I'm no match for you

170

even if I were to succeed in scraping together every last bit of my strengths."

"But my flaws are particularly terrible. I'm a grotesque mishmash."

"So am I."

"At my worst, I get so sick of my own hideousness that I just . . ."—she fished for words—"want to extinguish myself."

The expression touched a raw nerve with me. I had a dreadful foreboding that Kei, too, might begin fading away right before my eyes, and that there would be nothing I could do to stop it.

"Don't say such things," I said. I repeated, "Don't say such things."

Kei nodded. I could discern no dimming of her figure. As I continued to gaze at her, I felt happier and happier that she did, in fact, exist.

As we walked back to our building, I said, "I'd like to see your apartment."

"All right," she immediately agreed, but then fell silent for a time.

"Did you leave things in a mess or something?" I finally asked.

"Uh-uh."

"If it makes you uncomfortable, I don't have to see it today."

"What makes you think I'd be uncomfortable?"

"You got so quiet all of a sudden."

"I was going over the apartment in my mind. Your home can reveal so much about you."

"I want to know everything about you."

"I wonder if that's necessarily for the best. Don't you think sometimes people might be happier together if they simply let some false impressions stand?"

"Then I'll wait outside in the hallway while you plant seeds of false impressions."

"Nah, that's okay. I get my kicks out of pruning myself, but today I feel more like letting loose."

Number 305 was next to the large, three-bedroom apartment at the end of the hall, and I had guessed from outside that it must be one of the small, single-room units with a tiny kitchen-dinette. Even for a unit like that, the rent in this part of Tokyo was steep. Perhaps her parents were helping out by sending her a little extra money each month.

What did they think about their daughter remaining unmarried at age thirty-three? Did they know about her burn?

Though I supposed they had to, her parents did live after all in a faraway farming village an hour from the nearest city, and she could probably hide a lot of things from them if she chose. She might have decided to keep the fact from them for fear they'd start trying to meddle in her life. Not that it made any particular difference to me whether her parents knew.

"After you," Kei said after unlocking the door.

"Are you sure you don't mind my barging in like this?"

"I already told you: it's fine. It'll take the air conditioner a while before you feel anything, but it's just as hot out here in the hallway, so we might as well go on inside."

Stepping in, I was surprised to discover that the apartment was Japanese style, with a tatami-mat floor.

"I didn't know they had tatami apartments in this building."

"I think this is the only one left. There used to be more."

"They wouldn't have been rentable as office space."

"Right. That's why the others have all been converted."

"I'd pictured a Western-style room, with a bed taking up half the room," I said.

As I started to peer into the tatami room for a closer look, Kei spread her arms to indicate the kitchen and dining space just inside the door.

"This is my tiny little dining room."

"You keep it very tidy."

In the middle of the brown vinyl floor of the dining area stood a small, white laminated table flanked by two white chairs. The old-fashioned indigo fabric of the thin round cushions placed on the seats of the two matching chairs looked somewhat out of place.

"I have some barley tea in the fridge. Shall we have it in here or in there?" she said.

"Let's go on in there, if you don't mind."

"Sure."

In the tatami room, a cheaply made white-laminate wardrobe and chest of drawers stood side by side against one wall, and a simple, country-style foldaway table sat in the middle of the room. I had unconsciously envisioned an apartment outfitted according to my more middle-aged sensibility; seeing the unmatched, somewhat juvenile furnishings, it dawned on me that Kei was still just a girl. The discovery was quite endearing.

But perhaps I was jumping to conclusions. A woman without a lot of money could ill afford to discard the furnishings she had purchased in her twenties; she could not readily redecorate according to new tastes acquired in her thirties. The fact that a twenties sensibility and a thirties sensibility coexisted in a room did not necessarily indicate that the occupant had a girlish streak.

As I slowly took in the rest of the room, two remarkably large reproductions hanging on the opposite wall caught my eye.

"Those're what I was most nervous about," Kei said the moment she saw me looking at the pictures. She had been watching me from the kitchen as she poured the barley tea. Her tone of voice sounded more playful than nervous.

Both reproductions were of paintings in the Japanese *nihonga* style.

"I like *nihonga*," she said. "Everyone else seems to like the European Impressionists or American Modernists. Me, I definitely prefer *nihonga*."

"Seison Maeda?"

"You recognize it?"

"It has his seal."

"And you could decipher it?"

"I've seen this one before."

"The actual painting is this huge," Kei said, spreading her arms wide and smiling.

The painting was of a samurai warrior lying in a stone

coffin. But the mood was not dark. The artist had painted the interior of the coffin a bright, bold crimson, and this combined with the ornate armor the warrior wore created quite a dazzling effect.

"Who did this one?" I asked, indicating the second painting.

"That's a Seison, too."

"What's this supposed to be about?"

"That's the one I was more embarrassed about."

A number of men in traditional Japanese dress, presumably from the Edo period, stood over the naked figure of a young woman lying on her back. The men looking down on her on the near side hid from view all but the woman's breasts.

Kei came up beside me carrying two glasses of barley tea on a tray.

"What do you think they're doing?" she asked.

"I notice that two of the men have their hands folded, like they're praying."

"It's an autopsy."

"I see. So they're dissecting her."

"I like it a lot. But I was a little afraid of what you might think."

Perhaps the composition of the painting—a naked woman surrounded by a group of men—did say something about Kei's sexual inclinations. But it was nothing compared to the lecherous fantasies men had. The fact that the painting showed only the woman's breasts, the very part of the body Kei so stubbornly concealed, seemed more telling to me. In no way did the picture strike me as obscene; there was a sense of restraint and tension throughout, and it was genuinely a thing of beauty. I supposed something could be made of how both paintings depicted corpses as objects of beauty, but I did not really care to psychoanalyze.

I sat down to the barley tea Kei placed on the foldaway table. As I lowered myself onto a cushion covered in a summery, sky-blue flower-print, I felt once again like a middle-aged man invading the private realm of a mere girl.

I noticed that she had a compact stereo system.

Feeling a little ill at ease, I asked her rather lamely if her musical preferences were also nativist.

"Puccini."

"Ah."

"I'm partial to one particular song."

"The opera, huh?"

"O My Daddy Dearest."

"I don't know it."

"I'll put it on for you."

Kei rose to her feet. Some thirty CDs were arranged neatly in a case on top of her chest of drawers.

"The opera's called *Gianni Schicchi*. But I don't really care for the work. It's this one song that I like. 'O my daddy dearest, won't you buy me the ring? If my love is in vain, I'll cast myself into the river Arno.'"

"It's set in Florence?"

"You get the prize."

The arietta began playing. It was lovely.

Still, the paintings, and now this arietta. Though no fan of psychoanalysis, I could not but notice a certain preoccupation with death.

Did her attraction to an older man like me derive from some sordid self-destructive impulse? Oh my daddy dearest, is it?

Suddenly she was throwing herself at me.

With lips locked, we fell to the tatami and quickly forgot the arietta.

Later that same evening, everything came to an end.

15

I needed to get to work on the second episode of the series. I'd been able to dash off the first with preternatural ease, and I expected the second to come likewise with no great difficulty.

But when I sat down to write at a little past seven, after sharing a light dinner with Kei (some microwave pizza, a bowl of instant soup, and a simple salad, in the warm after-glow of our amorous exertions), I found that I could not produce a single sentence. An hour sped by in seemingly no time at all.

Kei had temporarily put my mind off the incident in Asakusa, but now it repossessed me, and no dramatic scene I could conjure seemed vivid enough in contrast. I found it impossible to shunt that unforgettable experience aside and direct my attention to a comedy of manners about men and women who spent a hell of a lot of time playing billiards and tennis.

"This is bad."

It did not seem like the sort of impasse I could break simply by trying harder. The story that had developed prac-tically by itself didn't even seem worth thinking about now, and the characters I'd created struck me as utterly hollow.

At this rate, it wasn't unthinkable that I might fail to deliver the script on time. For a hotshot writer in high demand, that might not matter so much, but for a lesser-known one like me, it could prove fatal.

What to do? If I needed a co-writer, the sooner I asked for one the better. But what could I offer by way of explanation?

No one would believe the story about my parents. Should I feign illness? No, I needed the money. I'd already promised Kei that I would buy a car. The intercom chimed. Far from buying a new car, far from moving into a new apartment, I'd soon find myself hard up even for daily necessities if I didn't whip myself back into shape. The intercom sounded again. Who could it be? The producer of my series? He'd never gotten back to me about the first episode. Or perhaps he had, but I wasn't home? I'd been away from the apartment quite a bit without ever turning on the answering machine.

I picked up the handset on the intercom and was surprised to hear Mamiya's voice.

"Could I come up a minute?" he said.

I had no desire to hear of his doings with my ex, but I knew the whole matter would soon start to weigh on my mind if I turned him away.

"Sure," I said, and pushed the button to release the security lock.

I couldn't very well ask Mamiya for help on work I was doing for another broadcast, but maybe he knew an up-and-coming young writer who could take over for me. I could tactfully inquire about someone like that.

The intercom's chime sounded again. When I opened the door, Mamiya looked me sharply in the eye.

"Are you all right?" he asked.

Oh, so it's that again, I thought with a smile. He's been worried about my health ever since he ran into me at the hotel. If that's what he's here about, it's already taken care of.

"As you can see, I'm perfectly fine."

Mamiya stepped inside without a word and closed the door behind him.

I continued: "When you saw me at the hotel, I was really wrung out from something I'd gotten involved in. But that's all been resolved. I'm fine now. I know it must be astonishing to see me looking so haggard one day and so ruddy the next, but there's really no need to worry anymore."

"You looked terrible then." He stood looking at me without averting his gaze.

"As I say, that was then, this is now."

"And you look even worse now."

I felt a chill, but forced a smile.

"Even worse?" I asked, half to myself.

I casually raised my right hand and examined the palm. Then I flipped it over to inspect the back. It looked perfectly normal—not bony and ashen as I'd seen it before.

"Do I look that bad?" I asked, lowering myself onto a chair.

"Don't you ever look in the mirror?"

"Not since getting home a while ago. No, wait. I did glance in the mirror when I went to the bathroom."

"Then go and take another look." He sat down across from me. "I can't believe you're just sitting there as though nothing were wrong."

His words echoed Kei's.

But now my mother and father were gone. I'd watched them vanish with my own two eyes. Did they still have some kind of power over me?

"Tell me something," I said, dropping my eyes to my hands again. I certainly couldn't claim my hands were the picture of youth, but neither could they be described as skin and bones. "How do my hands look to you?"

"What do you mean?" he said, obviously puzzled by my question.

"Do they look bony and withered?"

He answered with a simple nod.

Did that mean, then, that my parents were still hovering about somewhere in the shadows, giving me an illusion of vitality even as they continued to drain the lifeblood from me? No, not my parents themselves, but rather the unknown power that had allowed them to return to visit me in the first place. Was that power still refusing to release me?

"There was a woman with you."

"A woman?"

"Last night, you had a woman here with you."

"You came by last night?"

I'd stumbled home and lost consciousness, but I did know that Kei had stayed by my side. If Mamiya had come, Kei would have answered the door. She hadn't mentioned anything to me.

"You looked so bad when I ran into you at the hotel, I decided to drop by late in the afternoon, when I had a break in my schedule. You apparently weren't home."

That would have been when I was in Asakusa.

"Then as I was going about some other business, I started to worry. Maybe you were home after all, but laid up in bed. Maybe you were too weak to even answer the door. So I came back around nine. This time I saw a light in your window. I punched in your number at the door downstairs, but you didn't answer. Fortunately, a guy came out just then, so I grabbed the door when he opened it and slipped inside. I came up here and rang your doorbell. You still didn't answer. Now I was really worried, so I started banging on the door and calling your name. A few moments later, a woman opened the door and told me you were sleeping."

I would indeed have been sleeping.

"When I said I was worried because you'd looked so emaciated at the hotel, she assured me you were just a little tired—and closed the door on me."

I had been sensing a note of hostility in Mamiya's voice every time he referred to the woman and it had started to annoy me. But if Kei had rudely shut the door in his face, I could understand how he might have felt.

"As I walked away, I had this odd feeling that something wasn't quite right. Not because you had a woman with you or anything like that. But something seemed queer, somehow. As the elevator started going down, it suddenly hit me that I had been able to see into your apartment through the narrow crack in the door. I'd seen right through the crack as if the woman wasn't there! The door was only open a crack, and she stood blocking that narrow opening completely, so I shouldn't have been able to see much of anything inside. But it was as though I had seen right through her, right through her body."

I didn't react visibly, but anger was welling up in me. Not at Mamiya. Nor at Kei. It was indignation at the unknown power that had made my parents fade away into nothingness right before my eyes. Was that power now going to take Kei from me, too?

Mamiya continued. "I knew it was ridiculous. My eyes had to be playing tricks on me. Still, I didn't think it was a good idea to leave you in that woman's hands. You'd looked like a walking ghost at the hotel, yet she insisted you were perfectly fine. Something told me I shouldn't believe her. So I came back today, just after noon."

Though I knew Mamiya felt bad toward me—in fact, precisely because he did—I would never have expected him to show so much concern about my well-being.

"As I was getting out of the cab at the curb, I saw you coming toward the sidewalk. The woman was with you. I hesitated to call out to you—not because you were with the woman, but because you were a changed person. You looked the picture of good health, and, if anything, I'd have said you'd put on some weight. Okay, maybe you'd had a really good night's sleep. Even then, how could you look so bad one day and so much better the next? I was flabbergasted.

"Just then, I noticed a man stand up near the main entrance, where he had been pruning some shrubs. 'That was Mr. Harada who just left the building, right?' I asked him; he looked like he belonged here and he was staring after you, too.

"'That's right,' he nodded. He was in fact the building manager. Then he added, 'Talk about spooky!' I looked at him and asked what he meant. 'That woman with him,' he said, 'she looked just like the lady who was in 305.'"

Of course she did. 305 was Kei's apartment.

"'You mean she doesn't live here anymore?' I asked. I couldn't see anything particularly strange about you being with someone who'd recently moved out. But that's when he told me."

Mamiya paused a moment, as if to heighten the suspense.

"He said the woman had killed herself near the end of July."

Don't be ridiculous. It's some kind of mistake. Apartment 305 was Kei's home for several years now. Saying the tenant of 305 killed herself amounted to saying Kei killed herself.

Mamiya was watching my face closely for a response, but I gave him none. It wasn't so much that I wanted to hide my response from him; I was trying to hide it from myself I did not want to be reacting at all to such a preposterous suggestion.

"I had no reason to make anything of it at that point," Mamiya said. "I mean, many people look like many other people. But I wanted to talk to you. Maybe I was worrying needlessly, but your recovery was simply too sudden. It seemed unreal. So I asked the manager to let me wait in the lobby. Neither of you had been carrying anything, so I figured you couldn't be going far. On the other hand, I had no idea when you'd actually return, and I started wondering again if I might be worrying myself over nothing. Then the manager invited me into his office. He said I'd be more comfortable in there because it was air conditioned.

"As I waited for you in his office, he told me a little more about the suicide. The woman had stabbed herself seven times in the chest with a knife. That's what the police told him, anyway. Her family came. The whole matter was dealt with in an orderly, quiet manner.

"The woman we'd seen with you looked so much like her that he blurted all that out, but before that he'd been careful never to breathe a word of it. The apartment was remodeled right away and rented out to a health foods company for its Tokyo office."

What did any of this have to do with Kei? Silently, I continued to resist the implications of Mamiya's account.

"Then the manager signaled toward the lobby with his eyes, and I peered out the small reception window to see you and the woman getting into the elevator. I rushed from the room and saw the floor indicator stop on three, so I raced up the stairs to the third floor and opened the door from the stairwell into the hallway, trying not to make any noise. The woman had just unlocked one of the doors and you were about to go inside. 'That's number 305,' the manager whispered behind me. 'It's scary how much she looks like the woman who killed herself.'

"This was all happening in broad daylight, so it almost seems silly, but I knew I had to get you out of there. I rushed up the hall to the apartment you'd entered and pushed the intercom button and started pounding on the door. The manager was with me, too.

"A young man came to the door right away, and I told him we wanted to see the two people who'd just gone in, but he denied that anyone had entered. 'That's crazy,' the manager broke in. 'We both saw them go in, just now!' 'Then come on in and see for yourselves,' the other fellow said, stepping aside to let us through. It was a small, one-room office, and we could see right away that no one else was there. Just to be sure, we checked the toilet and bath, too, but we couldn't find any trace of you or the woman."

Having recounted this much in a torrent, Mamiya looked me in the eye again. "Where were you?" he demanded.

"This woman who killed herself," I said. "Why did she do it?"

"She apparently had an ugly burn on her chest. Plastic surgery hadn't helped much, I guess, even after several operations. So she kept almost entirely to herself, and they think she probably just couldn't stand the loneliness anymore."

I closed my eyes.

"Her name was Katsura Fujino," Mamiya went on. "But on her lease papers for the apartment she had given *Kei* as the reading for the character *katsura*. Look. I borrowed a spare key from the manager. Why don't we go check out Number 305 together? You can see if it's the apartment you went into this afternoon."

"That won't be necessary," I said.

"I really think you should. It'll give you the strength to resist."

Resist what? Kei?

"I don't know if these'll do us any good," Mamiya said,

taking two rosaries from the pocket of the suit jacket draped over his arm, "but I want you to take one."

"Forget it."

"We can't forget it. Please."

"It's embarrassing enough that I've been duped. Don't make me verify it."

"You're being awful easy. It hardly seems like you. Why don't you tell me I'm talking nonsense? How could this be anything but nonsense?"

Mamiya knew nothing of my mother and father, so my ready acceptance of his horror story understandably caught him by surprise. But I had already accepted the inevitable. So recently had I been merrily planning a new life with Kei; so suddenly I knew I could never make it happen.

"All right, then," Mamiya said. "Let's get out of here. We need to get you away from this place as quickly as we can. You can stay at my house. Or if you don't want to do that, we can get you a hotel room."

I studied my hands. I had to assume that I still could not see their true condition. They did not look like skin and bones. They looked like the fleshy hands I had always known.

Clearly, Kei continued to exert power over me. Was she aware that she had been exposed?

I longed for a chance to at least say good-bye. Kei was right. I was happier with the false impression. I would have been happy living with Kei, believing, mistakenly, that she was alive.

"Come on. We can figure out what to do after we've gotten you away from here."

I nodded once and rose to my feet. Kei probably wouldn't appear while Mamiya was with me anyway. Not that I meant to shake off Mamiya, whose concern for me I didn't fail to appreciate.

"I need to turn off the air conditioner," I said.

"I'll get it."

I thought it might take him a moment or two to figure out the controls, but he promptly switched it off and strode to the door to wait for me. I took just my wallet from a drawer and slipped it into my hip pocket.

As I started putting on my shoes, Mamiya pushed the door open and stepped outside. I felt him stiffen.

I looked up. Mamiya stood frozen with the open door at his back, staring off toward the elevator. It's Kei, I thought. Kei was here.

"Don't come out," Mamiya hissed at me.

Ignoring his warning, I stepped into the hallway. Kei stood in front of the elevator, some ten meters away, gazing steadily in our direction.

She wore the white, sleeveless housedress that came down nearly to her ankles.

"Kei."

"Don't talk to her!" Mamiya cried. I doubted he had any profound basis for this admonition. Perhaps he was thinking of an ancient taboo against communing with the dead.

Kei was looking at me. Her eyes were like a serious schoolgirl's.

Mamiya was exhorting me not to talk to her. No matter how intimate we may have been before, now that I knew she was a ghost, I had to regard her as hostile. Yet, once we stood face to face again, I could not bear to think of her in those terms. This was the woman who had clung to my neck and prayed desperately for me. What would turning against her and driving her away as an accursed being accomplish, other than condemn me to an empty, joyless future?

"Kei, I heard your story," I said.

"Don't!" Mamiya shrieked. Raising his rosary over folded hands he shouted, hurling the words at Kei, *Namu Myoho Rengekyo*! Glory to the Supreme Law of the Lotus Sutra!

Hoping to annul the power of the incantation, I, too, lifted my voice: "Kei, we'll be together! I don't care what happens to me! My dear Kei!"

"Are you out of your mind?!" Mamiya cried, his rosaried hands still thrust out toward Kei.

Kei took a step toward us.

Mamiya quickly took a step backward and chanted once more: *Namu Myoho Rengekyo*!

She took a second step.

"Harada-san! What sect does she belong to?" Mamiya asked frantically.

"I don't think she's religious."

"How about her family, then? They must belong somewhere!"

"I haven't the foggiest."

"Would you not be so relaxed? This is really happening!"

My eyes remained fixed on Kei's, and hers on mine. Without ever shifting her gaze, she continued taking one step, then another, slowly closing the distance between us.

"She's coming closer," Mamiya cried, his entire body shaking. "She's coming! She's coming!"

"Stand back, Mamiya-san," I said, still watching Kei.

"But I've already got my back against the wall!"

Indeed, the seventh-floor hallway ended a short distance past my door.

"Don't worry. She won't hurt you."

Kei continued her advance.

Of course not, I thought. She's not going to hurt anyone.

Wasn't there some way for us to work this out? Wasn't there some way for us to live together?

She kept coming. Five more steps and she would be standing right in front of me.

Step.

I remained still. Why?

Step.

Why did I stand frozen to the spot?

Step.

Why hadn't I gone to her and taken her in my arms?

Step.

She faced me, only a single step away.

"Kei . . ." I said.

Her eyes were as cold as death. I had been searching them for signs of life as she approached, but even now, even at close quarters, I could discern no ray of warmth in them. They remained fixed on me in a frigid, icy stare.

Her unpainted lips moved, parting ever so slightly, as though preparing to speak. Then they began to form words:

"I'm sure you remember."

A deep voice. A voice filled with scorn.

"Remember what?" The venom in her words made my voice quiver.

"The night of the champagne."

". . . Huh?"

That would be the night I brusquely turned her away from my door. The daze of the blow dealt me by Mamiya had left me in no mood for social chit-chat. I had regretted my coldness almost immediately. I didn't really believe she would kill herself, but the thought had occurred to me, and I'd even gone so far as to look for a light in her window on a rainy night.

Now I knew. On that very night, Kei had stabbed herself in the chest, seven times.

"I'll drag you down with me," she hissed, pressing another step closer.

I reflexively fell back, but she immediately closed the gap again. Try as I might to hold my ground, I found myself pushed backward once more by the violent hatred emanating from her two eyes, glaring at me from only a few centimeters away. It was as if I'd been physically shoved.

Did this mean it had all been an act—a charade she'd gone through solely to destroy me? What had seemed so much like love—was it all motivated by hatred? Then it wasn't love that made her plead with me so to stop visiting my parents lest it kill me?

As if she'd read my mind, her eyes now turned mocking. "Naive man," she spat out.

No, this wasn't fair! A complete stranger declines your

invitation to share a drink, and for that you drag him down to hell with you? Madness! Even if life was always more or less like that.

My back was against the wall. I could retreat no further.

"Go on living, then," her eyes snarled. Or, more accurately, her lips did, but she now stood so close that I could see only her eyes. "You can *have* your precious little life."

Then you won't drag me down with you after all?

"Not won't," those same eyes said. "Can't. By the time you came out of the apartment, at heart you were no longer with me. Even as you mouthed those pretty phrases about staying together, your heart was far away."

Though I had not been conscious of this separation, her words somehow rang true.

So that was how it worked: she couldn't drain my life-blood unless I loved her from my heart. The laws of the other world were difficult to fathom.

"I will go now, without taking your life—but not because I care for you in the least."

I felt dizzy.

Suddenly she was moving backward, her figure receding as though gliding on ice. On her way toward me, she had punctuated her progress step by step, but her retreat came in a single swift motion that carried her nearly four meters away at once. It seemed she was already well on her way back into the realm of the dead.

Then I noticed something on the front of her white housedress.

A black spot appeared on her chest and began to grow.

No, not black, I realized as the color spread rapidly across the white fabric, but red. The red of freshly flowing blood. From the very chest she had been at such pains to conceal, gloriously red blood welled forth as from a living being.

The blood pulsed forth to a sound like a beating heart, and formed into rivulets as it streamed down the front of her dress.

I looked into Kei's eyes.

She stood motionless, as though in mute endurance of the spilling blood.

Then her figure began to fade. As with my parents, the end came swiftly. Moment by moment she grew more transparent, until suddenly I realized I was seeing only an afterimage. It lingered briefly like the shimmering of hot air, and then it too was gone.

The dimly lit seventh-floor hallway stood empty before me.

Not a single drop of blood stained the floor.

I heard Mamiya letting out a deep breath.

I could not move.

In spite of her parting words, spoken with such venom, I thought I had spied a note of sadness in Kei's eyes, a genuine sorrow of parting, in the last instant before she finally faded away. I was incorrigible.

16

The next twenty-two days I spent at the Tokyo National Hospital in Komazawa. I had grown exceedingly frail, half of my hair had turned gray, and my eyesight had been damaged as well. Day after day of intravenous feeding slowly did its work, but my recovery was never complete. When I tried on my pants five days before discharge, I still had to pull my belt two notches tighter around my waist. The collar of my shirt hung loose about my neck as well, and my complexion remained sallow. Visitors tried to comfort me by saying I had the aura of a mystic.

I was obviously in no condition to write for a television series. Seeing that I was hovering over the brink of death, my producer instantly realized that it would do no good to badger or punish me; without any fuss at all, he agreed to talk to a younger writer he knew about taking over from the second episode.

"He's young and he has a real feel for what's hot," the director of the series said when he came to see me at the hospital. "He may actually be the better choice for the material. No offense."

He was trying to offend me, of course, but since I'd caused them extra trouble, some meanness was inevitable.

I left the hospital in mid-September and moved directly into an apartment Mamiya had found for me near Kyodo station on the Odakyu line. For about the same rent, I had a little more room than at my previous digs. Mamiya and Ayako and Shigeki had moved my belongings for me.

That night I called Ayako to thank her for her help. I asked to speak to Shigeki, too, so I could thank him directly.

"Yes, please do," she said. "He really knocked himself out."

I heard her calling him to the phone. In my mind I pictured the house that used to be my home, too.

"How are you feeling?" Shigeki's voice asked suddenly.

"I'm doing all right," I said.

"That's good."

"I wanted to thank you for helping move my stuff."

"It wasn't that bad."

His manner of speech was the same as always, but I didn't get the sense that he wanted to get the conversation over with as quickly as possible. Perhaps his feelings toward me had softened a little, now that we no longer actually lived under the same roof.

"How about we go out to dinner sometime, just you and me?" I suggested, pushing my luck.

There was a brief pause before he answered, "One of these days."

It was probably about as good a response as I could hope for.

Two days later I set out for Asakusa with Mamiya.

"Are you sure you're going to be all right?" he pressed, worried that I might find the trip distressing. But I had already found closure on the emotional issues during my stay in the hospital. Neither my parents nor Kei would ever appear again.

As we emerged from the subway at Tawara-machi and strode along International Boulevard, I noted wistfully that summer had come to an end. Even amidst the fumes rising from the busy traffic I could smell autumn in the air, and the pedestrians on the sidewalk moved with livelier steps than at the height of the summer heat. A season had passed, and so, too, had my parents and Kei.

"Harada-san," Mamiya addressed me in his formal manner as we walked along.

"What?"

"You mentioned while you were still in the hospital that you wanted to make a trip back here."

"Yes, I did."

"Well, maybe I should have said something sooner, but I came to have a look at the place four days ago."

"Oh?"

"I didn't expect to actually find anything, but I thought maybe I should check things out first."

"I see."

"The place was an empty lot."

Hearing that made me feel alone—like I was falling voicelessly through an endless abyss.

"They apparently tore down an apartment building in May, and now they're getting ready to remove some of the surrounding structures to make way for a new building."

"So it's been an empty lot since May?"

"That's right."

From International Boulevard, we turned left onto the street lined with small shops, and soon the alley where the apartment building had stood came into view. To this point, everything looked exactly as it had on my previous visits. But when we came to the alley, the metal staircase and apartment building were nowhere to be seen, as Mamiya had found out.

Bounded by the dingy walls of neighboring buildings, the small lot stood empty and forlorn, overgrown with an entire summer's worth of weeds. In its own way, this profusion of growth in an area otherwise devoid of greenery made it seem almost as if we had stumbled upon an otherworldly place.

"I think you said they lived in the last apartment at the back, right?"

"Uh-huh."

"I made a guess and figured it must have been in that general area over there. I cleared away some of the weeds."

Mamiya led the way into the empty lot.

The weeds came up to my waist, but here and there they had been knocked over or trampled down, and they appeared dusty and tired from the long hot summer. Some uncleared rubble and empty drink cans scattered underfoot made it a little difficult to walk.

"Here," Mamiya said, coming to halt. "I thought it might have been around here."

His hunch had been accurate. Directly beneath where the apartment I visited would have been, he had torn away the weeds to make a small clearing and had placed two cinder blocks on end—like grave markers.

"I found those lying over there and decided to make good use of them," he said.

"The apartment was on the second floor, but this is right about where it would have been," I said. "You did a good job of figuring it out just from what I told you."

Mamiya lowered to the ground the department store shopping bag he was carrying and lifted out a small bundle wrapped in newspaper.

"I brought some incense and a holder," he said.

"Actually, so did I," I said.

"I guess I should have told you I was bringing one."

"That's okay. We can set them side by side. I'll light some incense in both."

I opened the cloth bundle I was carrying and took out my own incense and burner—along with a small bouquet of chrysanthemums wrapped in newspaper. It had been two years since I'd last visited the family grave in Aichi where my parents' ashes were buried.

After starting the incense with my cigarette lighter, I divided it between the two holders, then brought my palms together in prayer. Mamiya did the same.

Oh! I thought. Next time I come, I'll bring the chopsticks my parents used at their last meal. I'll burn them and say another prayer for them. Now I have an excuse to come back, Mom, Dad.

"I suppose this is an odd time for me to bring this up," Mamiya said, "but I'm thinking I'd like to marry Ayako around the beginning of next year."

"I see."

"I suppose it might give you kind of a sour taste in your mouth, but . . ."

"No, no, not at all. It's true I felt betrayed at first, but now I honestly hope everything goes well for you two."

"Do you think you and I might be able to work together again sometime?"

"I'd like that."

"Let us then. We'll put together something really special."

"I'd like you to know," I said, "how genuinely touched I am by the concern you've shown me. I never would have expected it."

"I guess it's just that I've always been very fond of you," Mamiya said. "One thing led to another and I grew fond of your wife as well."

"That's where I might say you went a little overboard. But seriously, I wish you two the best."

"I can't help thinking there must be something seriously wrong with anyone who'd want to break up with such a wonderful woman."

"Really? As for me, I'd say there must be something seriously wrong with anyone who wants to marry a woman like her."

"And I suppose that's pretty much the way it is all around. When you get right down to it, we've probably all got a little something wrong with us. At your old apartment building, I witnessed something quite beyond belief, but when it was all over, there wasn't a single drop of blood left anywhere in the hallway. So it couldn't really have happened. That's how I see it. Something came over me that night and I just wasn't in my right mind."

"Huh."

"Let's just forget about it, okay? Otherwise, I don't know how I can go on living. I just wasn't in my right mind that night. And the whole thing with your parents, too—please don't get too caught up with that. You just weren't in your right mind either—that's all."

"I suppose you're right."

"Definitely. You were nuts."

I chose not to contradict him.

But I did not honestly believe that there had been anything wrong with me at all.

Good-bye, Mom. Good-bye, Dad. Good-bye, Kei.

Thank you so much.